D1446702

**I wanted to search Kastor's room, but not at the risk of getting caught…**

I heard a pounding on the stairs and spied an oversized head curtained with lanky, orangey hair rising in the stairwell. A heavy set of chins slung like necklaces over a pair of boxy shoulders materialized next, followed in turn by pendulous breasts, wide hips, and thick ankles.

As soon as she reached the landing, she lumbered down the hall toward me.

I froze long enough to notice nesting in her cleavage on a long, silk cord an L-shaped latch lifter with an iron shaft and a couple of teeth on the end.

The wide sleeve of her robe caught on a splintery doorjamb. I hoped that would slow her down. But it didn't. Her sleeve ripped instead, and she kept on going.

As soon as she entered the first room, I eased Kastor's door closed until I heard the latch click.

A drop of sweat trailed down my back and turned to ice. I pivoted on my heels and rushed to the trunk. I lifted the lid and plunged the candle into the darkness to see what was there. No sense sticking my hand in without checking, right?

But I could feel her footfalls shifting the floorboards and hear their groan. She was already at the door, working the latch. Stunned by the moment, I didn't know what to do.

My heart kept punching inside my chest. I looked

around conscious of only my own confusion. And then I dropped the trunk lid, pitched the candle into the chamber pot, and ran to the window.

I had no choice.

She'd lifted the latch.

To my friend, Addie

Miriam bat Isaac, a budding alchemist in first-century CE Alexandria, welcomes her twin brother Binyamin home to fight his last gladiatorial bout in Alexandria. But when he demands his share of the family money so he can build a school for gladiators in Alexandria, Miriam explains that he forsook his share when he took the gladiatorial oath. When she refuses to loan him the money for what she feels is a shady, and dangerous, enterprise, Binyamin becomes furious. Soon after, the will of Amram, Miriam's elderly charge, turns up missing; Amram becomes seriously ill; and the clerk of the public records house is murdered. Could Binyamin really be behind this monstrous scheme? If not he, who could be responsible? And is Miriam slated to be the next victim?

Best,
June
02/25/18

KUDOS for *The Deadliest Sport*

In *The Deadliest Sport* by June Trop, Miriam bat Isaac welcomes her gladiator brother home to Alexandria in 56 CE, not expecting the man he has become. Filled with anger and greed, her brother seems like a stranger. When odd things begin to happen, including the murder of a former servant, Miriam must discover the culprit, even though she fears what the answer may be. The story has a ring of truth that is rare in historical fiction, and it is clear that the author knows her history. A really good read. ~ *Taylor Jones, The Review Team of Taylor Jones & Regan Murphy*

*The Deadliest Sport* by June Trop is the story of Miriam bat Isaac, a liberated woman in Alexandria in the first century CE Her brother, who is a gladiator, has just returned from abroad and wants to open a gladiator school in Alexandria. But he has no money, having given up his share of the siblings' inheritance to become a gladiator. When Miriam refuses to lend him the money for what she feels is an unwise investment, he becomes angry and threatens her. Then people start dying, and it falls to Miriam to find the killer before more innocent people die. *The Deadliest Sport* is filled with well-developed and realistic characters, plenty of tension, and

an intriguing mystery, as well as a strong authenticity that was a real treat. This is one you won't want to put down.
~ *Regan Murphy, The Review Team of Taylor Jones & Regan Murphy*

## ACKNOWLEDGMENTS

I am grateful to the following people for their interest and advice: Professor Jean Lythcott, my mentor and inspiration; Professor Lewis M. Greenberg, scholar of Greek and Roman art and culture; Len C. Ritchie, my patient web designer; and Gail Trop Kushner, my own twin sister and first reader.

Finally, I want to thank my new friends at Black Opal Books—Lauri, Jack, and Faith, for believing in Miriam's story and working so hard to bring it to you.

# The Deadliest Sport

## A Miriam bat Isaac Mystery in Ancient Alexandria

June Trop

A Black Opal Books Publication

GENRE: HISTORICAL FICTION/HISTORICAL THRILLER



THE DEADLIEST SPORT

Author photo by Michael Gold, Corporate Image
Cover Design by Jackson Cover Designs

Print ISBN: 978-1-626947-55-9

First Publication: OCTOBER 2017



Published by Black Opal Books **http://www.blackopalbooks.com**

DEDICATION

*To my Paul*

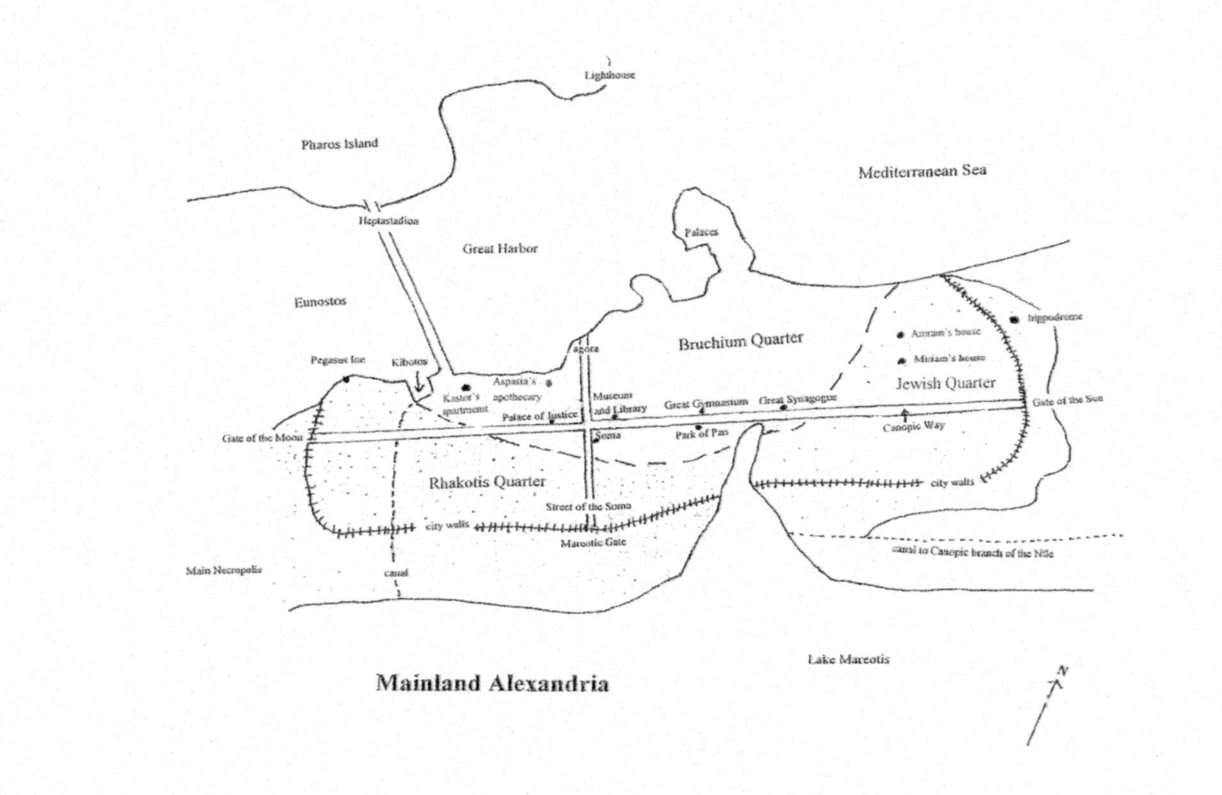

Mainland Alexandria

The Second Year of the
Reign of
Nero Claudius Caesar
Augustus Germanicus
(Nero)
56 CE
Near the End of
the Sailing Season

# PART 1
# MIRIAM'S STORY

"Deliberate violence is more to be quenched than a fire."
~ Heraclitus

# CHAPTER 1

*Friday (Shabbat) Evening, September 24th*:

How different my life might have been if my twin brother, Binyamin, had not come back to fight his last bout in Alexandria. But he did. And so I can trace the beginning of my horror and the indelible despair that followed to that Shabbat evening three years ago when, in the dying twilight of early autumn, I approached the pilastered entryway of Amram's mansion. That evening, we were to celebrate Binyamin's safe return after ten years as a gladiator from the famous *ludus* in Capua, the gladiator school Julius Caesar founded, the school that owned Spartacus more than a hundred years ago.

Our host, my late father's life-long friend, had become with the advancing years more my charge than my business partner. Amram had never been young, but since the Pogrom, when he lost his beloved Leah and their two daughters, sadness had pinched his lips, yellowed his cadaverous face, and engraved deep lines in his forehead. Then, with the death ten years ago of Noah, his only son and my betrothed, his skin withered like old parchment, and his once-lacy Hebraic beard dwindled to a tangle of errant whiskers spiraling out of a receding chin. A knee-length, rumpled linen tunic—not quite clean—had always engulfed his spindly frame, a heavy leather belt cinching the bulk around his skeletal waist, but that evening, his fleshless arms and legs poked out of the ripples of fabric, their joints swollen into nasty red knobs and their skin blotched with eggplant bruises. And most disturbing of all, his filmy gray eyes gazed out from deepening, mauve-ringed hollows.

I remembered that evening, walking the few blocks in the Jewish quarter from my family's townhouse to the opulent fortress that Amram had built after the Pogrom. Wrapped in the quietude of Shabbat, I heard only the rasp of crickets, the swish of leaves, and the song of night birds as the moon-cast shadows of cypress and plane trees stretched across my path. A drowsy breeze sifted through the branches licking the dampness off the nape of my neck and flapping the hem of my blue ankle-length, short-sleeved linen tunic, the white *tunica interior* I wore underneath, and the soft woolen himation that enveloped me. Binyamin would join us later.

Picking my way along the winding crushed-shell walkway, I wove around the frowning foliage and twitching boughs of the wasp-infested plane trees that shade the mansion. Myron must have spotted me through the grid that covered the porter's hole because he emerged from his cell as soon as I reached the box hedge that framed the portico and opened the thick, iron-studded door to welcome me. His bullish frame, narrow-eyed face, and wooden expression made him the perfect doorkeeper.

After taking my himation, he ushered me to my favorite perch in Amram's atrium, a padded stone bench beside the pool of floating lotus blossoms. Turning and adjusting my gaze, I took the moment as I usually did to admire the beds of dark blue irises and the rows of alabaster statues bearing lamps of eucalyptus oil. Then, sitting down, I smoothed my hair, tucked the flyaways under the gold-threaded braid that encircled the crown of my head, and pinched my cheeks for a little color. An instant later, two maids appeared—one to remove my *calcei*, my Roman boot-like shoes, and wipe my feet with a damp towel, the other to place before me a small mahogany table and serve me a goblet of Palestinian wine mixed with honey-sweetened water.

As soon as I'd refreshed myself with the wine, waggled my toes, and slid them into a pair of slippers, an old friend of Amram's, an Alexandrian businessman I hadn't seen since I left Caesarea eight years ago, glided across the onyx-tiled floor, fastidiously groomed and meticulously dressed in an emerald silk robe that trailed in his wake.

"Good Shabbat, Miriam. I hope you had an inspiring *Sukkot*," said Gershon ben Israel, referring to our Feast of Booths. The thick, silver tufts overhanging his intensely blue eyes bounced with enthusiasm just as they had when I first met him. We'd both sailed to Caesarea as guests of my cousin Eli on his ship, the *Orion*. "I wouldn't have thought it possible, but you're even more beautiful than when I last saw you. Your hair is the same chestnut brown; your eyes, the same crystal-clear blue—"

"And I have the same easy blush," I added, curling my hand around my neck as if that could staunch the telltale tide.

"—But now you carry your height with regal elegance. Your father used to brag about you, you know. He'd say you look just like your mother, that you have her softly-fringed, jewel-like eyes, delicate features, and translucent alabaster skin. I see that the eighteen-year-old woman I knew in Caesarea has become, like wine, more precious with time."

He paused, and then his voice thickened slightly. "My condolences on your father's passing. I knew him from the Great Synagogue. He was a man of unwavering principles, a bulwark of decency."

How kind of Gershon to characterize Papa's intransigence that way. But Gershon never saw that rigid side of Papa, or if he did, he was too discreet to mention it.

Gershon still spoke like an aristocrat, his speech as unhurried as ever, but his voice sounded unnaturally loud, as if he were addressing an audience. At the time, I thought he just might be excited about being here. Only later did I learn that the desert's Khamseen winds, those hot south winds that streaked the hard blue sky with grayness and choked us with their dust, had scorched him with a fever that burned out much of his hearing. Otherwise, the years had not diminished his charm, nor his loose-limbed grace, his trim, broad-shouldered athletic build, or his luxuriant cap of pearlescent curls, which he wore freshly oiled and styled in the latest Roman fashion.

Only the ruffles draping his jowls and the dewlap under his chin, hanging lower than I remembered, attested to the passing years.

"What a delightful surprise!" I exclaimed. "Amram never told me you'd be here for Shabbat."

"Pardon?" he said as his right hand pressed the rim of his ear forward.

"For Shabbat. I'm just surprised to see you. I didn't know you'd be here," I said, raising my voice and enunciating each word with an exaggerated precision.

"That's because I didn't know myself," he said as he

opened his verbena-scented hands, palms up, spreading out his long delicate fingers.

The swish of fabric was the only sound as Gershon folded into the seat beside me. He plucked the skirt of his robe as he crossed his legs and faced me, his amethyst seal ring momentarily stealing a spangle of light from an oil lamp when he clasped his hands and rested them on his knee. Then he explained:

"You may remember I buy grapes from the vineyards on the northern Plain of Sharon, and then, after their vinification, I have the wine bottled and shipped here to our upcountry brethren in the villages and towns along the Nile and to our own community of Alexandrian Jews."

The Jews in Egypt willingly paid the price for a wine from the Holy Land, one that hadn't been filtered on Shabbat.

"But as a special favor to Alexander when he was the procurator of Judea and then to his successors, Cumanus and Felix, I've been shipping the finest—and most expensive—of all wines, Faustian Falernian, that sweet white wine from the central slopes of Italy's Mount Falernus. And I trust only your cousin's shipping company to transport that wine. Other shippers would be only too glad to steal my cargo and substitute a cheaper wine with a counterfeit label."

I nodded even though I was getting tired of listening to his earsplitting voice.

"Well, that was my plan for the season, to shepherd the Falernian wine to Caesarea and from there, my Palestinian wine, which is really the heart of my business, to Egypt. But Eli refused to take a chance on shipping my cargo from Italy. 'Another spate of piracy along the Anatolian coast,' he said, waggling his head in resignation. 'And even if by some miracle you live through the attack and make your way to Judea, don't count on surviving the religious and political turmoil there, let alone conducting your business. Any member of the *Sicarii*, that secret brotherhood of Judean assassins, his dagger hidden inside the folds of his cloak, would gladly elbow through the crowd to slit your throat along with anyone else's he suspects of collaborating with the Romans. "Greek Jews," that's what those bloody militants call us, you know. Any Jew flush with a few Roman coins and he tops their list of faithless traitors.'"

"So you canceled your plans," I said in an effort to wrap up the conversation. Any mention of the *Sicarii* still conjures up that deadly terror I experienced in Caesarea, so much so that right then and there I felt that familiar spasm ripping through my bowels. Besides, I was anxious to see Amram. And where on Earth was Binyamin? So I adjusted my skirts and shifted my weight to signal I was getting up.

But Gershon lifted a silky palm to detain me. So, despite my mounting impatience, I sat back and folded my hands in my lap to resist the impulse to pick at the threads of my tunic, something I did whenever I felt edgy.

"Yes," he said, "but I decided too late. In anticipation of my absence, I'd arranged for contractors to renovate my home. By the time I canceled the trip, they'd already delivered the materials, and I'd dismissed my servants for the duration. So I arrived on Amram's doorstep like a homeless beggar until they complete the work."

I saw the smile in his eyes before it curved his lips.

"Well," he said, throwing up his hands before rocking forward, rearranging his limbs, and rising to his feet, "I'm sure the unrest in Judea is temporary. What would this world be coming to if Rome couldn't put down a few peasant uprisi—"

At that moment, a team of boots pounding on Amram's walkway bruised the quietude. The volume intensified until the cadence ended with a thud, and the crunch of a single pair of boots advanced toward the portico. I wheeled to my feet. Who would violate the sanctity of Shabbat by coming here in a litter?

The quick, firm tread of my brother's deerskin *calcei* and the jingle of their silver buckles followed Myron into the atrium. Etched with the scars of violence, Binyamin reeked of power, his body still flaunting its unbridled sexuality, despite the thickening of his midsection and the softening of his jowls over the years.

He was elegantly dressed in a tunic of the finest

Scythopolitan linen worn girded at the waist with a heavy leather belt studded with Alexandrian glass beads in the design of a trident and net, the tools of his trade. Didn't he realize the tattoos on his face, legs, and hands identifying him as the property of his *ludus* were enough to rank him with those despised even more than pimps and actors?

But unlike me, Binyamin had always flouted convention and slashed at boundaries. Our Aunt Hannah said he was reckless because, having been born breech, he blamed himself for our mother's death from childbed fever. And so he was forever tempting the Fates to settle the score. But whether or not Binyamin blamed himself and whether or not that guilt motivated him to sign on as a gladiator, Papa always blamed him.

"Hey there, everyone. Good Shabbat," Binyamin said as he tossed his chlamys, a sporty traveling cape, onto the bench. After an introduction, he extended his hand to Gershon and greeted me with an indulgent smile that told me he'd come only to please me.

Gershon, an aficionado of the games, blinked slowly for a moment before recognizing my brother as Agrippa Fortitudo, the combatant in Caesarea who slew Orcus, the highly favored and most popular gladiator in the Empire. Then pursing his lips and lifting those silver tufts, he spoke in a whirl of words.

"Why, you were hardly more than a *novus auctoratus*, a new hire! I couldn't believe it! You chose the perfect moment to trap Orcus and close in on him. All that despite your own blood staining the sand." Gershon mimed throwing the net low and aiming a trident at Binyamin's right arm. Then, glowing with the excitement of every sports fan reliving a tense competition, Gershon sucked in a breath and blew it out in a soundless whistle.

"All four tiers of us in the stadium were on our feet, stunned into silence, you know, as Orcus, our undefeated darling, was losing his hold on the freedom promised with a victory that night. Then the shouts, the thunderous explosions of '*Missum*!' (Let him be sent away') and '*Mitte*!' (Let him go free') the spectators calling for Alexander to spare Orcus's life. Why he didn't, I'll never know." Gershon waggled his head as he tucked his upper lip inside his lower one. "Instead, Alexander turned his thumb out, you had to plunge your dagger into Orcus's chest, and another wretched life ended before its time. Your sister and I were sitting with Alexander in his *tribunal* that day, you know."

Gershon shook his head ruefully and then continued. "Soon enough 'Charon' appeared with his long-handled mallet." At this point, the volume had leached out of Gershon's voice. "He struck Orcus on the forehead, and a team of *libitinarii* lifted him onto a bier and carried him away. I tell you we all cried, those of us who could believe our eyes, that is. The rest just stood frozen in disbelief, their faces convulsed, their skin pale as a fish's belly."

With his chest inflated, his head tipped back, and a spark of pride igniting his half-closed eyes, Binyamin showed me he too was reliving the romance of that bout. A few moments later, the spell broken, he strode to the bench, and sitting there long enough to change into his sandals and toss his *calcei* to Myron, he took up whistling a bawdy Roman tune. I snared his eyes and shot him a sour look, which he countered with an impish gleam and a bite on his lower lip in mock humility. Then he reached over to the mahogany table to wipe his face on my towel and drain my goblet.

ଓଃଓଃ

"Miriam, is that you?"

Amram's voice was like a feeble echo from another world. But no, he was as close as the doorway between the atrium and the smaller dining room, misery in the curve of his back, his fingers bent at arthritic angles, his body propped against the shoulder of his strapping, new full-faced manservant, Leo.

Alarmed by his frailness, I saw he was thinner than he'd been since even last Shabbat. I greeted him with a false heartiness and re-introduced him to Binyamin, whom he hadn't seen since long before Binyamin left for the *ludus*. Binyamin had rarely joined our two families at the Synagogue, except if he wanted to tease a girl there. He couldn't sit still long enough for the reading of that week's portion of the *Torah*—The Five Books of Moses—but more to the point, he was jealous of the attention Papa would lavish on Noah.

We joined Amram at the doorway and received his kiss before entering the spice-scented calm of an oval room softly lit by a rising Shabbat moon. We stretched out, each of us on one of the four silk-cushioned dining couches that together surrounded a low square table covered with an Indian cotton cloth. Set upon it were knives of various sizes, ivory spoons with carved handles, and silver ladles for the sauces. Flanking our couches were marble stands bearing Jerusalem clay lamps for burning oil on Shabbat.

Binyamin reclined across from Gershon, I, across from Amram, with Leo sitting on a stool nearby ready to assist him. The only other furniture in the room was a long, curved citron sideboard attended by two servers, Taharqa, a gangly, wild-haired Nubian, his skin more bronze than ebony, and Rho (for Rhoemetalces), a burly, olive-skinned Thracian with Asiatic features.

After Amram's blessings over the wine and bread, freshly baked from wheat flour and served with spreads of olives, chickpeas, and chopped egg, the conversation rambled from our recent Holy Days to the hopes we had for our people, especially our poorest brethren in Judea. But once Taharqa and Rho served the filet of mackerel poached in garum, I concentrated on the food, hardly listening as Gershon and Amram shared memories of their earlier days at the Great Synagogue and their opinions of Felix's administration of Judea.

My attention snapped back during the meat course though when Binyamin asked about a recent uprising, a topic hardly conducive to a peaceful Shabbat, one that left me nettled by his indifference to our ways.

"Remember when that so-called visionary from Egypt—another one of those stiff-necked Jews' self-appointed messiahs—well, remember when he gathered some twenty or thirty thousand believers on the Mount of Olives? So what did our mighty Felix do then?"

The fingers of both hands curled around his goblet, Binyamin looked over its silver rim at Gershon when he asked the question. Then he took a deep gulp, wiped his mouth with the back of his hand, and brandished the goblet to signal for more.

"Well," Gershon answered, "you know it isn't easy for Rome to deal with these false messiahs, especially when they're continually rising up all over Judea promising to deliver our people from Roman oppression. Terrorists, that's what they are though, terrorists and fanatics who, posing as agents of divine justice, do nothing but rouse the foolish hopes of the peasants."

Gershon's voice, vibrating with emotion, filled the room and stirred the curtains. The rest of us stopped eating, hardly daring to swallow until nothing could be heard but the hiss of the oil lamps and the buzz of a fly diving in wide arcs around the sideboard.

The tips of his impossibly long fingers moved with the precision of dancers as he rotated his goblet, raised it, and took a sip of wine before continuing.

"And then there are the unemployed shepherds and mercenaries, the brigands and the escaped slaves, the beggars and the resistance fighters. These peasant soldiers lurk in the countryside lying in wait behind a boulder or in a ravine, cave, or grotto poised with their clubs and slingshots. Ready to ambush the unsuspecting, they add yet another hazard to travel, as if sandstorms and sunstroke weren't enough."

He raised his goblet again, as if to take another sip, but then put it down.

"What I mean is this strife only exacerbates the very economic crisis these rabble-rousers accuse the Romans of fueling. No, it isn't easy, but the Romans are doing the best they can to maintain the peace."

But Gershon hadn't finished.

"And as for this false prophet from Egypt, Felix's troops did what they had to do. They hacked him to pieces along with his disciples till there was nothing left but a crimson fog for the flies, gobbets of flesh for the vultures, and a field of bones for the jackals."

The poached mackerel rose up my gullet.

Binyamin, his thumbs hooking onto the edges of his plate as if they carried the memory of a choppy sea, dropped his head. Still, I could swear his mouth had tightened into a self-satisfied smirk. I nudged him and pelted him with an angry look. Quick to retaliate, he flashed me a defiant grin that wriggled the boyhood scar on his left cheek. So I turned my eyes to Amram, who was twining a few strands of his beard.

Then, wincing as he leaned on one hand for support, he sat up to speak. “I agree, Gershon. The brutal power of Rome has stripped our brethren of their dignity and drained their economy. But that’s not what these uprisings are about. No matter how many thousands of patriots Felix cuts to pieces, our brethren will never accept foreign rulers in the very land the Lord set aside for them. For them, resistance is a religious duty.”

Since the Pogrom, Amram had avidly followed the politics that affected our Jewish communities.

A rill of saliva ran down Amram’s chin. Leo jumped up with a napkin immediately, but Amram dismissed him with a brush of his hand and wiped his chin himself as he drew in a wheezy breath. He had more to say. “Did Alexander’s crucifixions…deter anyone?”

When Amram was tired, he had to grope for the right word as if his memory had already fallen asleep.

“On the contrary, now the…Zealots and the…*Sicarii* are better organized than ever. And don’t forget: Felix’s…predecessors, with all their brutality, achieved only a partial and temporary success at best.”

Panting out his last words, a feverish dew gathering on his forehead, he wagged a crooked index finger before relapsing into the couch cushions.

An uncertain silence hung in the air, the kind after a door slams, and I wondered *where is the peace of Shabbat now*?

The stillness eased with the raspy call of a short-eared owl, and the conversation resumed, drifting among the standard topics, from Hero's latest invention to Philo's interpretation of the *Torah*. But interest in one topic or another quickly faded between Amram's long breath and suppressed yawns. While Taharqa cleared the dishes and whisked away the crumbs, Rho brought us a tray of tiny cakes flavored with ground locust and a pot of mint tea. Binyamin pawed a few cakes while we waited for Rho to serve the tea.

But I could see Amram, his eyes closing and his head falling forward, was exhausted. So I got up, murmuring an apology for cutting the evening short and thanking Amram for his hospitality. Binyamin, after an indolent stretch, extending his arms with a deep sigh and then lacing his hands behind his head, was quick to follow.

When Leo went to fetch my himation, Binyamin's chlamys, and our *calcei*, Binyamin caught my shoulder in the atrium and spun me around.

"What's with the looks tonight, Sis? I came here for you. You know this isn't my kind of party."

"Did you really have to come in a litter?"

"What's it to you? He's not the High Priest, you know."

"Binny, Binny, Binny. It's a matter of respect, to

Amram, the neighborhood, our people, our traditions. Surely you could have walked the few blocks from home."

"You know, Sis, I'm beginning to think I have no home, certainly not here. It's like I'm dealing with Papa all over again." He turned away and then with a sigh and a drop of his shoulders, which I interpreted as a drop of his defenses, he looked at me again, his eyes wide, his brow raised.

"Oh, forget it. Just ride home with me. I kept the litter waiting for both of us."

"No, Binny, I can't. I'm sorry, I just can't." And I felt uneasy, wondering whether his homecoming, an occasion I'd wished for, even prayed for, was going to be such a good thing.

And that longed-for homecoming, I had to remind myself, was only yesterday, a day that really began when Orestes brought me the news that Binyamin's ship was coming into port.

# Chapter 2

Thursday Morning, September 23rd:

She's coming into port, Miss Miriam, that's what the herald announced. The *Serapis*. Isn't that Mr. Binyamin's ship?"

"Yes, Orestes, and isn't it a perfect day to greet a ship!"

Having slept fitfully, I'd been up early that morning exchanging songs with our summer warbler while studying a rare succulent fern brought to me from an open field in Anatolia. My colleagues called this plant "the white herb of the mountain"—now known as *Botrychium lunaria*—and believed that when gathered by moonlight, it had magic powers. I'd been trying to determine whether an extract from its fan-like leaflets could be the basis for the elixir, the potion the League of Alchemists had asked me to pursue for healing, rejuvenating, and extending human life. When I heard Orestes's voice, I put my reagents aside, got up from my workbench, and watched the young sun brush color back into the world and gild the walls of Papa's study.

In my mind, this small square room off the atrium with its great mahogany ceiling-high doors was still Papa's. I suppose that was why I did so little to change it, except to set up a workbench along its eastern wall and get rid of that life-size bronze of my mother he'd commissioned a sculptor to fashion shortly after her death.

I certainly didn't remember her that way. In fact, I have no memory of her at all, only a longing, especially when I'm troubled, to breathe in a mother's consoling scent and experience the comfort of her arms around me.

No longer able to concentrate on the fern, I moved to the armchair in the center of the room behind Papa's massive ebony desk. I swiveled to my right and aimlessly poked the beads of the abacus, watching them roll back and forth in the grooves cut into the marble top of its antique table. Then, turning around every few minutes, I looked behind me past the purple tied-back drapes to peer into the peristyle. I'd gauge the length of the shadows its columns were casting and wish, by willing them to shrink, I could advance the time to Binyamin's arrival.

But no, the morning would wear away at its own pace, even if it took an hour for each minute to pass.

"As soon as you're ready," Orestes said, "Solon and I can bring out the sedan chair and take you to the harbor."

Papa bought Orestes and Solon ages ago to transport him through the city in a style commensurate with his status as a promising young investment banker. Despite the passing years, both bearers had remained strong, top-heavy men with huge, veiny hands and thick, ropy necks. But of the two, I preferred the plucky, needle-eyed Orestes—my kindred soul—to the phlegmatic, sleepy-eyed Solon. When not in our outbuilding buffing the leather cushions of the sedan chair or waxing its carved mahogany supporting poles, each was available to me as a handyman or bodyguard. And with Binyamin home, they'd be available to him as menservants.

I myself rarely used the chair, preferring to walk instead, but I did take one of them with me whenever I went into the residential district to our southwest. When Alexander the Great recognized in our two-mile-wide strip of limestone the potential to become his great city, this neighborhood was the fishing village, pirates' nest, and old Egyptian outpost known as *Rhakotis* or Building Site. But today, the *Rhakotis* quarter was the pitiless underbelly of our otherwise splendid city, where the Egyptians who worked on the waterfront, in its shipyards, warehouses, and quays, still lived.

Papa would joke that even the mosquitoes went hungry there, but the fact was we both learned the hard way how dangerous crossing into that pestilential quarter could be, even in broad daylight. "Corpses surface in the canal there every morning," Noah used to say, "and no one seems to care who's beaten or left for dead in the streets." Once he told us about a woman who was raped there. Afterward, so she couldn't accuse her attackers, the fiends gouged out her eyes and severed her tongue.

"I won't need the chair, but come to think of it, Binyamin could probably use help with his luggage, and I'd feel more secure with you alongside me once I enter the *Rhakotis* quarter and head toward the *Eunostos*, The Port of Good Return."

The *Eunostos* defined the northern boundary of the *Rhakotis* quarter. This smaller and more western of our two harbors was the port of exchange with other cities of the Mediterranean, the interior of Africa, and the Orient. The canal, the very one Noah mentioned, putrid, stagnant, and lacy with scum, connected the *Kibotos* or Box, the small, square artificial port inside the *Eunostos*, to Lake Mareotis and eventually to the Canopic branch of the Nile.

And so that morning I was spurred by the energy of anticipation, my heart hammering and my ears buzzing, my legs sometimes skipping to keep up with Orestes, sometimes his scissoring to keep up with me. The sun was almost overhead by then, pricking through my parasol, pouring over my skin, and coating my throat with splinters. What's more, as the sun's fire baked into the cobbles, the heat seemed to melt through my *calcei* and scorch the soles of my feet.

"Which way first, Miss Miriam? West or north?" I didn't have a chance to answer before he said, "North. Fewer crowds. Let's go north."

He decided against pressing westward through the cloying beggars, gawking tourists, and sweat-soaked street philosophers that choke the Canopic Way. The Way, as we called our longest and most impressive boulevard, ran five miles from the Gate of the Sun in the east to the Gate of the Moon in the west. Lined with porticoes and colonnades, monuments and statues, sphinxes and temples, even its one-hundred-foot-wide pavement would be clogged by the camel caravans, chariots, mule-drawn wagons, groaning oxcarts, rumbling drays, sedan chairs, and curtained litters, never mind the usual cohort of legionnaires with their hobnail boots scraping against the granite rectangles.

So we threaded north instead and then west through our Jewish quarter toward the shoreline of the *Bruchium* quarter, the Palace Area, where the gentle slope of the land and the briny essence of the sea reminded me of the strolls Aunt Hannah and I would take every Shabbat afternoon. She and I, after passing the barracks and armories of the Roman fleet, would linger on the beach to catch the gentle breezes as they skimmed off the water.

And then we'd listen to the sea, the caws of its gulls, the tolling of its buoys, the voices of its ships, and the rhythm of its sighs.

But with no time to dawdle, Orestes and I forged ahead, past the palaces and gardens along the base of Point Lochias, the promontory of royal land that belonged to the Ptolemies and where the Roman governor now lives. As soon as we passed a broad span of beach, a brisk sea breeze rushed across the water, curling the breakers, awakening the drowsy air, and coaxing our way the resinous smoke from the perpetual fire atop the Pharos Lighthouse. Having withstood the ravages of storms and earthquakes for more than three centuries, the sight of this nearly four-hundred-foot, triple-tiered, marble-faced tower has always comforted me. As lost as I might be, my position relative to its lantern could always guide me though the city's maze. And so the sight of its billowing smoke that morning reassured me that Binyamin's ship would arrive safely.

We followed the coastline along the Great Harbor, the circular bay a mile and a half across that was both a public harbor and the port for Roman warships. Once I smelled the fried onions that season the neighborhood around The Flamingo's Tongue, a favorite restaurant named for its signature dish, my heart began to flutter with the kind of expectancy that precedes the realization of a long-awaited dream.

In contrast, Orestes's pace eased. His tread became

more buoyant, and his arms relaxed into a graceful swing. We were almost there. As soon as we could twist our way through the warren of lanes spidering out from the *Kibotos*, we'd be at the piers of the *Eunostos*.

I scanned the scores of ships gliding toward the quays. Pulled by a harbor tug manned by burly rowers, each split the current and curled the water in its wake. And each wafted the odor of burnt flesh from its poop deck, where the captain performed a post-sail sacrifice in gratitude for a safe arrival.

But the *Serapis* was moored by then, the passengers already trudging down the gangways, rocking on their sea legs, swiveling their heads, and squinting into the distance while the gulls dipped and wheeled overhead to greet them. And the bare-chested, brown-skinned stevedores, slick with sweat, had begun unloading the goods we regularly receive from all over the Mediterranean: gold, tin, and silver from Spain; wine, pottery, and animal hides from Gaul; and honey, copper, and statues from Mainland Greece to name just a few of the luxuries destined for the shops in the agora.

Rather than count the barrels, amphorae, sacks, and crates, something I felt compelled to do years ago before Papa and I reached that understanding about my future, I directed my eyes to the river of faces on the gangways and the multicolored blur of costumes on the wharf. Searching for Binyamin through the blazing spikes of sunlight and the swooping wings of gulls, I called for him over their mournful cries only to gulp the fishy tang of the harbor instead.

"Look! That's Mr. Binyamin," said Orestes, roofing his brow and pointing into the distance.

"Where? I don't see anything!"

"He's coming this way. Can't you see him?"

Later Orestes told me he hadn't actually recognized Binyamin. He'd just noticed two men, an odd pair but apparently together, spilling down one of the gangways, their faces, arms, and legs marked with tattoos; their bodies virile; their postures aggressive. The burly one, wearing a coarse, gray woolen tunic, his thickset arms hanging away from his body, had a long, leathery face scored with savage lines, hands like huge grain scoops, and feet like enormous flatfish. So Orestes figured the other one, who was dressed in a gaudy, Chinese silk tunic, crimson with a geometric border print embroidered in gold, must be Binyamin. He was too tactful to mention that the one in the flashy tunic was also lambasting a shame-faced, bowlegged porter for being rough with his luggage, something we could both imagine Binyamin doing.

A few moments later, in the flurry of greetings, Binyamin introduced me to his beefy companion, a comrade from their *familia gladiatoria*, their troupe of gladiators. They'd sailed here together, each to fight his last bout in Alexandria before being discharged from their *ludus*.

"Just think, Sis, in two weeks, Tychon and I will be released. He's from Caesarea, but he'll be staying on to be a *doctor*, a gladiatorial trainer for me at the *ludus* here. I have big plans—wait till you hear them—to take over that pigsty and expand it into something we can actually be proud of."

Tychon stretched his lips into a satisfied smile and dipped his head.

"You remember Sergius, right, Sis?"

Who could forget Sergius, that outlandish ex-gladiator who fled to Alexandria with Eppia, the senator's wife who'd given up everything, her several hundred slaves, her villa in Rome, and her seaside estate at Antium, to be with him? Still the favorite of gossipmongers, he was the subject of abounding rumors, that he'd been seen here or there, at the theater or the games, our clearly recognizable popular hero with a stump for a right arm, a dent in his head, a wart on the end of his nose, and an ichor trickling from his swollen eyes. Word had it that the senator was still searching for them. But more to the point, acting as the agent for Rufinus, the *lanista* or manager of Binyamin's *familia gladiatoria*, Sergius recruited Binyamin and financed his voyage to Rome and then his trek to Capua.

"You remember him, right?"

"Of course."

"Well, he's gonna negotiate a deal for me to buy out the owner of that dinky, poor-excuse-for-a-*ludus* we have here. In the meantime, Tychon will be staying at The Pegasus. Sergius must have something going with the *cauponaria* there, the innkeeper, because she's agreed to let Tychon a room, board and prostitutes included, all gratis. I can only guess how Sergius pays her."

That quip and a jab with Binyamin's elbow forced a guffaw from Tychon, one of the few times I'd ever hear his voice.

"Well, good buddy," Binyamin said as he slapped Tychon on the shoulder. "You're all set. The Pegasus is straight ahead, right on the waterfront. Just follow this strip of warehouses—" Binyamin pointed toward the western end of the port. "—until you see the inn. The sign out front shows Pegasus springing from Medusa's womb. So go, make yourself at home, and I'll catch up with you later."

Tychon picked up the threadbare, draw-string pouch at his feet, slung it over his shoulder, and without so much as a good-bye, shuffled off, disappearing into the dust of a graffiti-lined alley strewn with garbage. Only then, daring to disturb the air, did I let out a breath. I'd never have admitted it, but in the sweat fermenting under my arms, I could smell my fear of Bin yamin's savaged-faced companion.

A moment later, Orestes looked at me and jerked his head in the direction of home. I gave him a nod, and after wiping his hands on the skirt of his unbleached, knee-length tunic, he lifted Binyamin's trunk, a monstrous rattan crate with Iberian leather straps and brass trimmings, and bracing it on his shoulder, carved his way toward the *Kibotos*.

I hadn't been alone with my brother since we took that one last extravagant spin around the city in the litter I'd hired to mark his departure for Rome. I was certainly not counting that dreadful encounter in the *hypogeum*, that labyrinth below the arena in Caesarea, the air of its tunnels, chambers, and cells thick with misery, fear, and death. Besides we were hardly alone, and Binyamin was puking his guts out.

No, our last opportunity to communicate was when we'd folded ourselves into the curtain-lined litter and cruised high above the ox dung, carried by the polished ebony bodies of eight Nubian bearers, their starched white tunics threaded with gold. Right then and there, as we lounged on the overstuffed cushions scented with rosewater, I gave him our mother's fibula, the one our father had given her upon their marriage. Having once belonged to Papa's grandmother and then his mother, it passed to me when our own mother died.

A symbol of our father's love and the future of their family, the fibula seemed to embody a mother's protective spirit, exactly what Binyamin would need in his new life.

The metallic screech of a lone gull diving for a glossy fish jolted me back to the bustle of the wharf. With Binyamin and me standing in an awkward silence, staring at each other like strangers, I couldn't resist a gibe at his companion.

"So, where'd you find *him*?" I asked rolling my eyes toward the alley.

"Who?"

"Come on, don't play dumb. That charming companion of yours."

"Oh, don't be like that. He's been a good friend, the only one in the barracks who ever helped me. Rufinus, the *lanista*, put me in Tychon's cell because he speaks our dialect, if he speaks at all. You'll see. He's kind of quiet. Remember, I was only sixteen. You know the minimum age is seventeen, right? I got accepted only because Sergius vouched for me—"

And my brother thought I was the one who was naïve.

"—so, I really needed a buddy. Anyway, Rufinus must have figured as long as he spent the money, he might as well see I was taken care of. So maybe he told Tychon to watch over me, or maybe Tychon just did it on his own."

"Well, thankfully you're home now."

"Say, Sis, let's walk along the Way. I know it'll be jammed with every rag picker and pickpocket even with this brutal sun staring down at us, but I wanna see the sphinxes again. Remember how we used to ride them like horses?" He rocked back and forth on his heels, his neck arched, releasing bubbles of the same boyish laughter I'd hear when we were kids. "And let's pass by the Gymnasium. Remember my first bout? I thought Papa was gonna have a seizure right then and there."

How could any of us forget Binyamin's first bout of *pankration*, a strenuous sport that combines boxing and wrestling. As a fourteen-year-old just beginning his ephebic training, he inadvertently killed his classmate. After an equal exchange of jabs and solid body punches, Binyamin caught the golden-haired Titus in a strangle hold that dropped him to the mat before he could surrender. After that, Papa treated Binyamin even more harshly.

Binyamin broke into a soulless laugh.

I expected him to unroll his long-standing chronicle of grievances against Papa right then and there. Whenever he did, the stories would consume him until his voice, choking with rage, would break into a trail of coughs.

"Sure, Binny. Let's see if kids still ride them."

He waited to regain his poise. Then he took in a deep breath, let out a sigh, and told me more about his companion. As it turned out, a lot more.

"Initially Tychon was condemned to the arena for three years, a sentence no one could be expected to survive. See, when you're a prisoner-of-war, slave, or criminal, you're just thrown into combat without any training or medical care. But by the time I joined the *familia gladiatoria*, Tychon was already a *veteranus*, a gladiator trained, experienced, and valuable. He'd not only survived his sentence, but he'd begun his first of two five-year contracts as an *auctoratus*, a hired gladiator like me, a professional."

"So what was his crime?"

"Murder. He killed—"

"Binny!"

"I know it sounds bad, but just listen. He killed a publican in Caesarea, some slime named Vibius Arrius Corvus who'd bid successfully for the post of tax collector. One day, this tax collector had the soldiers seize a boy and scourge him for crying out when he saw his father bound to the wheel and mauled for not paying his taxes. As Tychon tells it, both the father and son died a few hours later right there in the forum. And no one even dared move their pulpy bodies." Binyamin's voice sparked with outrage. "You should have seen them: their eyes swollen shut and the pavement littered with hunks of their flesh, tributaries of their blood, and twists of their excrement."

Just when I longed for a fresh breath, I felt the muscles tighten around my chest.

"You know every tax collector has bodyguards, right? But Tychon, just a seventeen-year-old street kid, had the courage and cunning to waylay Arrius Corvus when the bloodsucker thought he was alone under his own portico. Anyway, that's my buddy."

As we crossed the Street of the Soma, our other

thoroughfare, I noticed a bunch of wide-eyed, copper-skinned boys following us, shrieking and jumping as if on springs, courting Binyamin's attention to no avail.

"So as Tychon tells it, the tax collector, when he returned to his estate after an evening at the Upper Palace, dismissed his bodyguards, bearers, and the *pedisequi* who accompanied his litter. Then, just as he called to his doorkeeper, that's when Tychon slid out of the shadows and strangled him with his bare hands. No surprise. He was apprehended immediately and condemned to the arena."

I wondered whether Binyamin admired Tychon as much for his scruples as his cunning and brawn.

"But once Tychon's sentence was up, Rufinus offered him a contract to train as a *secutor*. Not everybody's husky enough to carry all that armor, you know, beginning with a huge rectangular shield and a smooth, close-fitting helmet. Add on a metal arm-guard, a greave for his left leg, and, of course, a sword, and we're talking maybe thirty-five, forty pounds easy.

"Believe me, if Tychon hadn't had the physique to be a *secutor*, the court would have condemned him directly to the wild beasts. He'd have been tied up, thrown to the lions, and any scraps of him left on the arena floor would have been dumped into the sea."

I don't know whether it was the glare of the midday sun, my having tossed half the night spiraling in and out of fearful dreams about Binyamin, or his granite face and uninflected tone when speaking of such wanton brutality, but my knees turned to liquid, the horizon lurched, and for the moment, I had to cling to his arm for support. But Binyamin just continued to prate, impervious to my distress.

"Anyway, you know I'm a *retiarius*, right? From when you saw me in Caesarea."

I would have nodded if a greasy glob hadn't rolled up my gorge. All I could do was keep swallowing.

We'd been dodging a drove of pigs, zigzagging around their tuffs of dung, Binyamin's voice powerful even above the clang of smithies and the steady rasp of soldiers' boots. He was so engrossed in his story that he failed to notice not only the sphinxes but the Gymnasium's marble colonnade and its porticoes, each over two hundred yards long.

"And you know the most popular contest is between a *secutor* and a *retiarius*, right?"

This time I could nod. Not that it mattered. He was going to tell me in any case, even though I'd heard all about *secutores* and *retiarii* a hundred times before, whenever images of being a gladiator danced in his boyhood eyes.

"Well, that's because they're a perfect match. For offense, a *retiarius* has only a trident, a wide-mesh, circular throwing net, and a small dagger tucked inside his belt. Very little for defense, only some strapping around his left arm and, attached to it, a bronze shoulder guard that extends to his elbow. That's it. No leg armor, not even a helmet. But that gives him the mobility to keep the *secutor* at a distance, where the net and trident are most effective.

"But a *secutor* is the opposite. He has the protection of a shield and helmet but not much maneuverability. His shield is heavy, and his helmet, although smooth with a rounded top so the net can slide off easily, has only the tiniest eyeholes, too small for the points of the trident to penetrate—good for his defense, right?—but narrowing his field of vision and restricting his air supply. So the *secutor* has to get in close and finish the *retiarius* off quickly, before he tires from too little air. See what I mean about they're being opposites?"

I didn't say anything. I just wondered why he wasn't even interested enough to ask me about Aunt Hannah? Then I felt guilty for being critical of him, especially so soon after his arrival.

"Of course, Tychon and I would never be paired in actual combat. No *lanista* would risk losing two valuable *auctorati* in the same bout. And no *editor*—he's the organizer of the games—would risk having to pay the *lanista* for such a twofold loss unless the bout promised to be exceptional. See, even the victor can die from his injuries afterward, right? And that's why when gladiators train, with or without an opponent, they use only blunt weapons. So Tychon and I would train together with extra-heavy, wooden weapons in the small arena in the courtyard of the *ludus*. And that's when he'd give me pointers."

"Okay. So even though he's a killer, he's your friend because you practiced together and shared a—"

Binyamin began waggling his head before I could even finish my sentence.

"There you go. I knew you wouldn't understand." He threw up his hands. "Look, the *ludus* is a savage brotherhood. Tychon and I took care of each other. The guys can get pretty rough, especially on a young *novus auctoratus* like me. Anyway, every recruit, before he can train with a partner, has to practice on a six-foot wooden post to learn how to strike with the tip rather than the edge of his weapon. That way he can penetrate an opponent's armor without exposing his own right side. Well, my first day on the post, I was attacked by a *veteranus* who broke my collarbone. Tychon levered the pieces of bone back into place and then called for Albus, our trainer, to apply a healing unguent. Come to think of it, you met Albus in Caesarea, the gapped-toothed guy who led you out of the *hypogeum*."

"Okay, okay. I understand your loyalty to Tychon. I just found him repulsive. Besides, I'm a little jealous. I didn't know you'd be coming home with somebody. How come you answered so few of my letters?"

"Gee, Sis, you know I'm not good at that stuff. And to tell the truth, you wouldn't have approved of the life I was leading anyway. So why go into it?"

"Well, I hope we can spend time together, do some of the things we used to do, like go to the beach and take trips into the countryside. Maybe you'll even learn the mortgage business and help me manage our investments, once you settle in, of course."

"Learn the business? Are you kidding? Where'd you get that idea?" he asked, his voice rising to a shrill pitch, his eyes narrowing with incredulity. "Where were you, on Hesperus or something when I kept telling Papa I had no intention of counting money for the rest of my life? If I'd wanted to do that, I'd have stayed home and been the perfect son just like you were the perfect daughter."

He stung me with his sarcasm. And that was when I felt another greasy glob roll up my gorge, but this time the liverish slime coated the back of my throat. Yes, he'd come home, but he was still simmering with rage, harboring the same old resentments.

# CHAPTER 3

*Saturday (Shabbat) Mid-Afternoon, September 25th*:

"So how was dinner last night?" Aunt Hannah asked, her broad hips spilling over the cushions on her wrought-iron chaise. We were in the courtyard enjoying our customary Shabbat lunch together. When she turned her pillowy body to face me and unfolded an ample forearm to reach for the basket of pita, I'd have sworn she could see.

Blind since birth, Papa's younger and only sibling had always lived with us. Still, even with the lifeless chips of jade that camouflaged as her eyes, Aunt Hannah saw more than most. As a co-conspirator rather than a parent to Binyamin and me, she helped Iphigenia, our slave of blessed memory, rear us to follow our dreams as she could not. Hers had been to marry her only suitor, our cousin Eli's father Samson, who'd started a shipping company to transport goods entirely by sea between the Mediterranean and China.

But my father and grandfather objected to the match. They suspected Samson was more interested in her dowry than her welfare, that he'd take her to distant ports along his trade route where they couldn't protect her, and that he might even leave her in one city to rendezvous in another with a client, or worse yet, a paramour. So they decided the family would be better off investing all of its capital in a business for my father rather than dividing it up to give my aunt a dowry.

And all the while, they carped that Samson's laugh was too loud, his nose too long, his palms too damp, his hair too greasy, his cologne too strong, his manner too familiar, and his tongue too glib. Still, it wasn't until I sailed to Caesarea, when I met Samson's son Eli, whom I likened to a lascivious, overfed gorilla—and an arrogant one besides—that I conceded my grandfather and father's objections might have been justified and finally forgave my father for depriving my aunt of her one opportunity to marry.

The sun had long since scaled the eastern wall of our limestone townhouse to paint a yellow sheen on the courtyard's tessellated floor and spin the lacy spray from the fountain into a shower of rainbows. Aside from the basket of pita, we were sharing a platter of sweet oranges, olives, and sliced hard-boiled eggs in a mustard sauce; a pot of black tea; and in celebration of Binyamin's return, a dish of our cook's famous candied almonds.

I poured the tea, watching it arc into Aunt Hannah's glass while she nibbled on an olive, her tiny yellow teeth like a row of corn kernels. A gentle breeze stirred the scent of the roses Papa had planted and rippled the leaves of the date palm and dwarf plane trees that dappled our table with their flickering shadows. At the same time, the hands of the breeze caressed our faces, fingered the folds of our tunics, and splayed the loose tendrils of my aunt's once luxuriant, caramel hair into a silvery halo. Her face was still smooth, with only a few lines etching her brow and fanning out from the corners of her eyes, but her legs had given in to time, their newly scribbled veins limiting her to hobbling around the house and only then with the help of Adonia, the Greek slave I purchased for her when I returned from Caesarea.

I put the teapot down. "What did you ask me?"

"About the dinner. At Amram's." Aunt Hannah picked up her glass and swallowed a sip of tea. Its mist pearled the hairs above her upper lip.

I coated a slice of egg with the mustard sauce, handed it to her on a wedge of pita, and watched her enjoy the burst of flavor. She wiped a drop of mustard sauce from her lips with a napkin. Then I took a slice for myself.

"You know, Auntie," I said, as the tang of the mustard sauce flowered in my chest, "the only thing I remember is Binyamin's behavior: his snide remarks, his coarse manners, his Roman haughtiness, his perverse sense of humor, and his wholesale dismissal of our traditions."

"That's quite a lot to remember." Sitting back, her elbows pressed to her sides, my aunt propped her chin on her fingertips and closed her eyes.

She remained silent as if scouring her brain for an answer while a fresh breeze rearranged her halo and snapped new folds in her tunic.

"In short," I said, "I'm worried about him, how he'll adjust to being home, whether he'll go back to being the Binyamin I once knew, the one who, thank the Lord, is still thoughtful enough to reciprocate the loyalty of a less fortunate companion. That's the brother I've missed, that sometimes naughty but often playful and always loving adventurer who encouraged me to stand up t—for myself."

I wondered whether my aunt caught my stammer, that barely perceptible hesitation when I almost said "stand up to Papa." Why upset her? She adored my father. He'd been her protector and provider ever since she was a little girl. As she used to tell me, he'd not only dote on her, taking her here and there, dropping her off at a friend's house and calling for her when it was time to come home, but he shared his music tutor with her and bought her a cithara, something she said calmed her other yearnings, something she enjoys to this day.

"Of course, I'd love for Binyamin to get married, even rear a family, but I'd be content just to have him join me in the business."

"I doubt whether he'd consider doing that, and you yourself learned when your father wanted you to marry Noah, the importance of being free to choose your own future."

Aunt Hannah picked up her glass and inhaled the full-bodied aroma of the tea.

"Oh, I know you're right, but this Binyamin is a stranger to me." I could have shed a thousand tears, but instead I bit down on the knuckle of my index finger to block the deeper pain inside me.

"Yes, Miriam, I can hear the loss gnawing at your heart." Her voice soothed me like warm honey as she reached across the table for my hand.

"Remember, Auntie, when I told you I saw Binyamin in Caesarea, first in the arena and then in the *hypogeum*? How I hardly recognized him, his body yes, still virile, still powerful and magnetic though it'd filled out some since he left Alexandria? He had the same thicket of ginger curls that the sea would plaster to his head when he'd tunnel through the waves, but his soul had changed, as if he were a Roman instead of a Jew."

At that moment, Binyamin's voice, imperious, vibrating with anger, and barbed with expletives, poured out of the windows of his suite, through the peristyle, and into the courtyard. As I wheeled around in disbelief, his words smacked me in the face.

"What do you mean you won't mop the floor?" Binyamin's tone thickened. "I don't care what day it is."

A stream of high-pitched whimpers, undoubtedly from one of our young housemaids, either Minta, who was a whirl of gleaming energy, or the shy, light-footed Calisto—I couldn't tell which—floated above his rant like the whine of a mangy dog.

Then he fouled the air with a chain of Latin curses, ones my beloved tutor, Hector, had refused to teach me.

He paused to take a breath, and when he spoke again, his voice was clotted with arrogance. "Who do you think you are, you lazy wench? I'm head of this house, not you. In case you didn't know, I give the orders around here. You'll do as I say or—"

Another wave of whimpers, these even more poignant.

"—I'll have you scourged and your torn flesh sold to feed the lions."

I could picture him, his teeth flashing, his eyes narrowed to viperous slits, and his face empurpled as lines of anger shot across his forehead.

Then I heard his door slam and the clatter of the maid's scurrying feet echo down the corridor and up the steps to the domestic servants' quarters on the second floor.

Reaching across the table, Aunt Hannah grabbed my arm and, gripping it like a vise, shuddered as if she'd caught a chill. Ten years away had certainly not improved Binyamin's temper.

# CHAPTER 4

*Saturday (Shabbat) Late Afternoon, September 25th*:

Lying on the cushioned mahogany sofa in my sitting room, I alternately held up a scroll of *The Odyssey* to catch a trapezoid of light from the wide, arched, east-facing windows and lowered it to gaze at the mural on my western wall. I was comparing the artist's rendering of the Sirens, perched on the rocky coast of their island singing their fatal song, with Homer's description. The afternoon heat had faded to a dull throb, and the dark leaves of the cypress trees outside my window were cutting the quiet rays of Shabbat into a feathery pattern across the mosaic floor.

I must have dozed for a time because when my eyes

fluttered open, I found myself curled onto one side, my palms pressed together as a pillow under my left ear. The shadows having inched past my marble-topped, wicker writing table, signaled that the afternoon was sliding toward dusk. I sat up, rubbed the sleep from my eyes, and reaching down to pick up the scroll unfurled across the floor, I saw the elegant, silver-buckled deerskin *calcei* I recognized as Binyamin's and smelled the sour stink of last night's henket, a cheap Egyptian beer made from barley or emmer wheat.

"Miriam, we have to talk."

"Of course, Binny. What is it?" Finger-combing the damp ringlets clinging to the back of my neck, I sat up and waved him toward one of the mahogany chairs flanking the sofa.

He sank into its cushions, rolled his shoulders back, and took a deep breath. Then he laced his fingers, pushed out his palms, and cracked his knuckles.

But he said nothing.

So I brought up the maid.

"I heard you shouting at the maid this afternoon. I think you frightened her."

"Frightened her?" he asked with a sudden jerk of his head, his face crinkling as if he'd suddenly smelled something putrid. "Look, all I did was ask her—okay, *tell* her—to mop up the dust from the unpacking I did this morning. What's so bad about that? You'd have thought I'd told her to—"

"—Binny, you know our tradition prohibits work on Shabbat, and for not just ourselves but everyone in our household, animals included. Shabbat is a day for spiritual renewal and illumination, for relaxation and study, a time for even the lowliest slave to be free."

He lowered his chin, closed his eyes, and pinched the bridge of his nose. Then, leaning forward and gazing at me directly, he said, "Honestly, I didn't come here for a lecture about Shabbat. I'm here to talk about my future."

He cracked his knuckles again. This time I heard them pop.

"You know I want to buy and expand the *ludus* here, make it into something really special. Can you imagine, one hundred *ludi* in the Empire, and ours is the shabbiest?" He waggled his head in disbelief. "A disgrace."

I couldn't imagine any *ludus*, let alone ours, but I nodded nonetheless.

"I wanna to tear it down and construct a three-story brick building to house about a thousand men. It'll have an inner courtyard with fountains, several small training arenas, and an amphitheater for about twelve hundred spectators with a separate grandstand for the most important guests."

He sketched a diagram in the air with his index finger.

"I figure I'll also need some outbuildings." He ticked them off on the fingers of his left hand: "A refectory and cookhouse, a medical facility with top Alexandrian physicians for the *auctorati*, administrative offices too, and quarters for the staff and slaves who'll be responsible for training the gladiators and running the school. Oh yeah, and a heavily-guarded armory for the protection of the *ludus*, especially from the *noxii*, you know, the condemned, who could start a riot or stage an escape anytime. That's five."

Suddenly, I tasted the mustard sauce welling up in my mouth.

"See, with a bigger *ludus*, we can hire out more gladiators, up to fifty pair for a single, four-day event."

"Sounds like you've got this all figured out." I said, gathering my legs, rocking forward to stand and end the discussion.

"Well, that's where you come in."

"Me?"

I sank back into the cushions.

"Come on, Sis. You know what I'm getting at," he said, leaning towards me still more, our noses almost touching, his palms spread out. "I want you, my loving sister and number one fan, to finance the—"

"Binny, stop right there. It's Shabbat. You know I won't talk business on—"

"There you go again, acting just like Papa," he said, throwing up his hands and spewing out his words in a torrent of bitterness. "You parrot the same inane rules he did, and just like Papa, you'll stoop to any ploy to block me from getting what I want." But a moment later, his face hardened, he mumbled something to his knees, rose to his feet and, cutting across the shadows, headed for the door.

"Wait, Binny," I pleaded to his back. "We can talk about your plans tomorr—"

But in my heart I knew I could never finance a venture that called for armed guards to keep desperate souls in check. Nor could Amram. All I could think of was the stench of fear and the groans of despair from those so miserably caged in the grisly cells of the *hypogeum* in Caesarea.

Nevertheless, weeks later, I would look back and pinpoint that late-September Shabbat as the day when the Fates began to close in on both of us and sow the seeds for the inconceivable tragedy to come.

# CHAPTER 5

*Sunday Early Morning, September 26th*:

Calisto eased the study doors open enough to poke her head inside. I'd just finished crushing the last of the fern's fan-like leaflets so they could soak in the various waters I'd prepared. Next I was going to cut up the cakes of dung I'd been drying in the courtyard. I figured they'd be a good heat source for my still, the one I invented years ago in memory of Noah.

"Mr. ben Israel is waiting for you in the atrium," she whispered, her mouth hardly moving, her sloe eyes sliding down her coarse, short-sleeved woolen tunic as she bowed her head.

In the milky light fingering its way between the

columns of the peristyle and into the study, she could see I was hardly ready to receive anyone. Still in my rumpled *capitium* despite the sharp, early morning chill, I'd spent the night entangled in an epic nightmare, watching helplessly from the arena's first tier as Binyamin-the-Roman snared Binyamin-the-Jew in his net.

"Miss Miriam, what should I do about your guest?"

"First ask the cook to cobble together something for him to eat. He's probably not had breakfast yet. Then bring me a damp cloth, a comb, and my blue cotton tunic. After you serve him, help me with my hair, and when you think I look presentable, I'll come out to greet him."

And I wondered what trouble could have brought him here so early.

ᘓᘐᘓᘐ

Gershon was fidgeting with his seal ring, twisting it back and forth and slipping it on and off his finger, but when he saw me, he slapped his hands on his knees and levered himself up from the teak bench facing the atrium's sunken marble pool. Carrying himself somberly, he zigzagged around the planters of white chamomiles and yellow field marigolds while the click of his heels filled the air and awakened the echoes in the atrium's vaulted ceiling.

He still had the bearing of an aristocrat, but the downy hairs on the back of my neck prickled when I saw his tuft-like eyebrows drawn together in a silver V aimed at the bridge of his nose.

"Gershon, you look uneasy," I said, as he grasped my cold hands.

"Yes, it was easy to get here."

"No, I mean you look upset."

He closed his eyes in a nod of agreement. "First, I must ask you to forgive my intrusion. I seem to be doing that to my friends lately." He struggled to smile but managed only a weak twitch. "Well, I wouldn't have come, especially at so early an hour, but I—"

His breath was so rank it reminded me of the matrons, chattering through their rotting teeth when we'd be crammed together in the Synagogue on the High Holy Days.

"Never mind that."

I had to repeat myself before he heard me. So I raised my voice. "You're always welcome here."

He nodded again, this time in gratitude, and followed me into the study. Unfastening the gem-studded brooch at his right shoulder, he opened his woolen cloak, a Tyrian purple *lacerna*, and took a seat in the chair fronting Papa's desk. I slid into the armchair but hinged forward with concern, my forearms resting across my thighs so the cushions couldn't swallow me up.

As he settled into his chair, crossing his legs first one way and then the other, clasping and unclasping his hands in his lap, I recalled sitting there myself when Papa would summon me for a rebuke. I'd cower as his eyes bored into me, feeling awash in shame and guilt for having failed him. But as Gershon sat before me with his shoulders hunched, I sensed he was carrying too great a burden to hold himself erect.

He pitched his gaze over my right shoulder toward the peristyle. I'd opened the drapes behind me so the early morning sea breeze could drive out the still-vivid memories of my nightmare. Perhaps their billowing folds caught his attention. Or perhaps his eyes lured him farther, to the peristyle's cascading ivy or the screen of boxwoods beyond its colonnade. He blinked a few times, squinting slightly to regain his focus, and then turned his head toward the courtyard where our summer warbler was enjoying breakfast in the expanding daylight. But when I shifted my position—I knew he wouldn't hear me if I merely cleared my throat—he turned back to face me, dropped his eyes briefly as if to consult his fingers, and then began in a voice thick with guilt.

"You heard what Amram said Friday night, that the uprisings in Judea signify more than a passing discontent. After Shabbat, citing the bloody battles that have marked our history along with the simmering confrontations of recent years, he made the case that our Judean cousins, imbued with pride, resolve, and above all, a sense of their own holiness, will fight to the death rather than subject themselves to the Romans or any other race of barbarians."

He shook his head as if to rub out the image. "I have to admit Amram persuaded me. That's why I'm here."

"I don't understand."

"Years ago your father and Amram, out of their long-standing friendship with me, invested in my business so I could expand the production of my Palestinian wine and export—"

"Yes, and we've done quite well thanks to you."

"But wait. Let me finish. You see, I no longer believe the Romans can restore the peace that's so vital to our prosperity. Quite the opposite. Of course, they retaliate as efficiently as they can, but how can they prevail against agricultural strikes when the crops are crucial and the tenants are willing to soak the soil with their own blood? And how can an army stamp out the terrorism in the cities, the banditry along the highways, and the guerilla warfare in the countryside? As Roman frustration seethes and their brutality escalates, the Judean peasants are becoming ever more unified, militant, and covert. That's why I now predict there'll be a full-scale war in Judea, maybe not this year or even the next but certainly within the decade."

The blare of his voice, on that morning sharpened by alarm, slashed my ears like the blade of a knife. I averted my eyes, as if that could dampen the shrillness, and clutched the edge of the desk, as if that could forestall the headache gathering across my eyes.

"And so I urge you and Amram to let me buy back your shares in my company—"

"Surely not, Gershon. That would cost you dearly."

"—and help you liquidate your other holdings in Judea."

"Are you certain? This all seems so sudden—"

"Oh, I was afraid you'd say that," he said, taking the moment to press his eyelids closed with his thumb and index finger. "But I assure you, and Amram will back me up on this, since Cumanus became procurator, and now, of course, with Felix, insurgencies have become endemic."

I wasn't so much afraid of financial ruin. We really had comparatively few holdings in Judea, but could I really trust Gershon's judgment when only two days ago he was so confident of Rome's ability to crush the uprisings?

"Listen, Miriam, I'm the one who encouraged Amram and your father to invest in, not just mine, but other businesses in Judea as well. So mark my words. When that economy collapses—" He dragged out the word "when" and jabbed the air with an impossibly long index finger. "—you at least might have time to recover—no war lasts forever—but Amram's another story."

"Oh no, Gershon, no." I was about to tell him that things wouldn't be so bad for Amram either, but he didn't give me a chance.

"And so, my conscience battered me all night. I kept asking myself: How could my well-intentioned advice to a dear friend have gone so awry? Why should a pious man, a kind and generous man, have to suffer more losses than he already has?" He balled his fists and pounded the desk while Papa's precious oil lamp, the glass one engraved with the asp, skittered across the desk and teetered on the edge. I used to stare into the eyes of that asp to avoid looking into Papa's when I was spinning a lie.

"Tell me, Miriam, where is the justice in this world?" His voice broke like a pubescent boy's over the word "justice."

"I don't know, Gershon. I just don't know," I mumbled, crossing my arms, and waggling my head.

I had to say something, but he probably didn't hear me.

"I just have no idea what his other Judean investments are, only that they're all at risk. That's why I need your help. You manage his affairs. So, after a sleepless night—" Gershon took in an anguished breath. "—I knew I had to see you." Then he knotted his hands and stared at them in his lap.

"What exactly do you want me to do?"

"Eh?" he said, raising his head to look at me.

"What should I do?"

"I want you to give me a list of Amram's holdings in Judea."

"Amram's holdings? In Judea?" I asked, scratching my head to feign perplexity but using the time to craft a lie, its germ already sprouting in my brain.

He looked leper-white even with the morning sunlight pushing past the drapes and catching the edges of his narrow brow. From his rapid, shallow breathing, I wondered whether he was suffering from an attack of mania brought on by too much bile in his brain. But even if I knew that his humors were balanced and his motives pure and even if I concurred with his assessment of the Judean political situation, I couldn't give him that information without Amram's permission.

"I suppose I've been remiss, but I have no such list," I said, while staring into the eyes of the asp. "Sure, I have access to the certificates and deeds, which Amram keeps in his private box at the Public Records Office, but I've never kept a list of them."

"Oh, but you must have something," he said, as if he'd read my mind.

"A few notes maybe, scribbled in a hurry, scattered here and there, but nothing I could lay my hands on, certainly not right away. And even if I found a few, how would I know I'd found them all, if, in fact, I could find any…" I let my voice trail off but was afraid my answer was already too long to sound convincing.

He didn't seem to notice, though.

"What you can do," I said, "is get the token from Amram and see for yourself what's in the box." I certainly wasn't going to hand over mine. "You know where it is?" I didn't wait for an answer. "The Public Records Office is inside the Palace of Justice."

"Sounds like a plan." His eyes shifted for a moment to the warbler, still in the courtyard, probing between the tiles with its small, finely pointed bill for another insect or perhaps a seed. "So, can we go tomorrow?"

"I'd rather send my bearer, Orestes, to go with you. There's a clerk there. He looks like an underfed jackal. You've probably seen him, the one with the clubfoot. Kastor. He used to be Papa's secretary, but we had to let him go. Oh, he was competent all right—he can read and write Latin and Greek perfectly—but years ago, we had to sell him to the civil authorities when we had a financial reversal. Ever since then, he's been unpleasant to us."

I certainly wasn't going to tell Gershon about Papa's gambling losses. Even Amram didn't know about them. "So, he left our household, ended up in a cramped, rat-infested *cella* in the *Bruchium* quarter, and never forgave us. I can count on him to be surly whenever he sees me. So if I need something, I send Orestes."

"Well then, it's settled. And I'm relieved you're willing to liquidate your shares. You won't be sorry. I promise."

Well, I actually hadn't said that, only that I wouldn't object if Amram gave him access to his documents. Besides, I planned to instruct Orestes to watch closely to make sure no one, not Gershon or anyone else, had an opportunity to add or remove anything from the box.

With that, we both stood. As he smoothed the folds in his garments, I asked him whether he wanted some tea before he left or perhaps some sesame cakes, porridge, or apricots. But he said no, he'd already taken up enough of my time and he'd let me know what he found. So, after an exchange of the usual pleasantries, I accompanied him to our porticoed entrance, where I watched the hem of his *lacerna* brush our stone steps and flash one last wink of purple as he rounded the corner of our two streets.

At the same time, I heard the rhythmic approach of a team of bearers, their swift light-footed tread tapping against the cobbles of our side street. I stepped outside beyond our portico in time to see Gershon swivel his head apparently astonished by such a garish litter, its canopy fringed with ostrich feathers, its voluminous curtains studded with beads iridescent in the burgeoning daylight. But then I noticed two shapely, feminine arms, a matched set, part the curtains. Stacked with bracelets, their long, thin fingers aglitter with rings and tipped with painted stiletto nails, they held the curtains open for my brother to bend over the side rail and vomit into the street.

I couldn't say why, but I ducked inside, noiselessly closing the front doors and slipping into the study. I hid there like a common thief, holding my breath, one hand clamped over my mouth, while I heard Binyamin cross the threshold and stagger down the marble-columned corridor, the slurred chant of a bawdy rhyme accompanying him until his door thudded shut.

# Chapter 6

*Sunday Late Afternoon, September 26th*:

I sent Calisto to Aspasia's apothecary shop for some mandrake root to relieve my headache. Whether it flared from Binyamin's wantonness or Gershon's dread, I couldn't tell. All I knew was my head was throbbing like a sore thumb. Upon Calisto's return, our cook expressed the juice from the bark and served it to me in a goblet of water. Then Calisto led me to my *cubiculum* where my body melted into a dreamless sleep. Awake and refreshed by late afternoon, I was back at my workbench cutting up the cakes of dung when I heard Binyamin's footfalls in the atrium.

He opened the study doors with a flourish and

dropped bonelessly into the chair facing my desk. Tilting his head back, he affected a bored attitude with windy exhales aimed at the ceiling while I took a minute or so to store the cakes in an earthenware scyphos, one of the full-bellied antique wine cups from my father's collection. Then I slid into the armchair behind the desk. But this time rather than lean forward, I settled into the cushions. I knew what Binyamin wanted. Besides, his animal stink hung over the desk like a fog.

Judging by his appearance—his jowls, chin, and neck dark with stubble; his hair matted; his tunic (last night's) grubby; and his face still stamped with rumpled bed linen—he'd just awakened. Pushing the oil lamp aside, he planted his elbows on the desk and hinged toward me, but I repositioned the lamp so I could look into the eyes of the asp. Then I stood, and balancing my right hip on the edge of the desktop, I lowered my chin to look straight at him.

The leaf-filtered sunlight drifting in from the courtyard illuminated the blotches of overindulgence that stained his face and the purple crescents that pillowed beneath his eyes.

"What's with you, Sis? Too uneasy to sit down with your own brother?" he asked, his eyebrows arched and his lips pursed to underscore his mocking tone.

"I'm wondering what brings you here before Orestes or Solon has even had a chance to shave you."

"What's the big deal? You told me to speak to you

after Shabbat about the *ludus*, right? Or did you think I'd forget? Maybe you just hoped I would." A sly smile played on his lips.

I said nothing. I simply perched on the edge of the desk, my head cocked like a bird's, while he quickly pushed out his words.

"Look, I know you don't approve of a gladiator's life, but it isn't so bad. Really, it's not. For someone trained like me, an *auctoratus*—I'm not talking about the others—I risk life and limb in the arena only two or three times a year. In exchange, during my first term I got food, shelter, clothing, the best medical care, and two thousand *sestertii* for each bout, more whenever I won, which was often."

I wondered how long Binyamin had been rehearsing this pitch.

"Hey, a legionnaire gets only nine hundred for a whole year, and he still has to pay for his upkeep. Anyway, now that I'm in my second term, I get twelve thousand for each bout. I don't have to be billeted at the *ludus*—I can come and go as I please—but, of course, I have to pay my own expenses. The real attraction for me, though, is living on the edge and having the chance to earn a place of honor in society."

"Maybe among the vulgar, but not among the people I know."

"What about Gershon?" he asked.

"Gershon included." But as soon as I said it, I knew I was wrong.

"You're dwelling on the slaughter, but people are used to that. They come for the showmanship. By accepting his death as a foregone conclusion, the gladiator lets go of all fear and fights with the determination of the desperate. That's when his skill and perseverance, his strength and courage earn him glory."

"No, Binyamin, you're not earning glory. You're cheapening human life."

"Okay. Have it your way, but you saw how a stunned silence gripped the stadium as soon as my net wrapped around Orcus's legs and how afterward the fans couldn't stop cheering."

"That's not the way Gershon tells it." I couldn't wait to get that in.

"Well, let's not argue. I'm here because Alexandria deserves a *ludus* better than the one it has, better than the one even in Capua. And who else should own and manage that *ludus*?" Angling toward me, he spread his arms, palms out, as if the answer was obvious. "With Tychon as one of my *doctores* and Sergius getting me others, I'll be able to buy, train, sell, and hire out my own gladiators."

He parted his lips and closed his eyes, as if anticipating his dream. "So, that's what I want to do. And with Papa gone, even you should have no objections. Not that he ever considered your feelings. Remember how he kept pressing you to marry Noah. Noah, who always toadied to him. I couldn't stand—"

"Stop it, Binny."

"Okay, okay. But Papa never considered my feelings either, and I'm going back, way back, long before even Titus. He never treated me like a son. All he ever did…"

His voice grew strident, his consonants harsh like metal scraping against stone.

I let him rant, but I couldn't listen to the same old grievances, like bubbles bobbing to the surface and bursting with that same old stink. Papa's tirades. Gusting with fury, his jaws clenched and his eyes flashing, he'd berate Binyamin, who'd stand there with his arms akimbo, his eyes fixed abstractly on the ceiling, and his lips compressed to hold back a retort.

Papa's harping on every fault, real or imagined, and then grounding him, except from school. Needless to say, Binyamin would have preferred the grounding to include school. Papa's refusing to enroll him in a *collegium iuvenum*, where he could have trained in the martial arts as a youngster. Papa's forcing him instead to become an ephebe. Papa's forbidding him to go to the games. And worst of all, Papa's continually comparing him unfavorably to Noah.

The litany went on and on but boiled down to Papa's unrelenting harshness no doubt fueled by his blaming Binyamin for our mother's death. Papa had honed that blame into a sharp-edged bitterness that wore smooth only when he realized he'd driven away his only son. But by then, Binyamin was on his way to Capua with a few sundries and all the sorrows of his childhood, its antagonisms, disappointments, and rejections, jammed into his travel bag.

Finally, when the energy had leached out of Binyamin's voice, he sank back into his chair.

"So Binny, what's stopping you? Surely not any objection I might have. You have Tychon, your connections through Sergius, your experience in the business, and a pile of money."

"That's just it, Sis. I have no money."

"How could that be? You yourself just said that between your scheduled earnings and your bonuses, you've done well."

But I knew. Binyamin has always been profligate. At that moment, however, I had only a keen desire to shame him.

"Well, it's like this. I owe Sergiu—"

I held out my palm to stop him and shook my head in feigned disbelief. "Wait a minute. That's impossible. Surely the *lanista* withheld the funds from your earnings to pay Sergius the money you owed him. I think you told me you'd owe Sergius half your signing fee and five percent of your earnings." I looked into the eyes of the asp. Actually, he never told me the exact figures, but I'd overheard Sergius when, in that seedy cook-shop in the *Rhakotis* quarter, he explained the terms to Binyamin.

"But more to the point, you also gave Sergius considerable collateral, your entire share of our mother's jewelry, including the Alexandrian pearls that were her dowry. So how could all that be gone?"

"Well, I guess I didn't explain myself clearly. A gladiator doesn't get to keep all his earnings. Most of it, seventy-five percent, goes to the *lanista* outright. So I didn't earn as much as you think. And then once I became famous, I couldn't stay in a shabby *caupona* with carters, sailors, and slaves. And you wanna know what else? I couldn't eat like a peasant. So before I knew it, my living expenses had swallowed up my earnings, and I had to borrow against my collateral."

"And gambling?"

"A little of that too," he said ruefully as he waggled his hand.

My imagination fired up a momentary image of him sitting with burly ruffians at a table marred with gashes in the dimly lit backroom of a squalid inn along the *Via Appia*. Drunk, his face carpeted with stubble, he was engrossed in a dice game about to risk our mother's pearls to buy a few trinkets for his whores.

So I asked, "And whores? I suppose you needed money for that too."

"Gee, Sis, you're wrong about that. Albus would find women for Tychon and me and then unlock the gate so they could wait for us inside the exercise grounds. That's when a key really comes in handy." Along with a lewd gesture, he exploded into a guffaw that blew his foulness in my face. "The women would flit toward us like moths to a light, but every once in a while, I'd tip Albus anyway. I'm sure he was grateful."

"So what's left after all these years?"

"Not much, just our mother's fibula. Remember you pinned it on me? In the litter on our way to my pier. To protect me while I was a gladiator. But the gift was only temporary, right? I knew it really belonged to you."

I nodded. Yes, I'd given him the fibula right then and there, two days after he'd concluded his business with Sergius, but I never realized he appreciated my attachment to it. Aunt Hannah once told me that when our father gave it to our mother, they dreamed of their eldest daughter wearing it someday.

Who knows? It might have saved my life a decade ago when beaten by thieves, I lay like a pile of rubbish in an alley beside an old slaughterhouse in the *Rhakotis* quarter. That's when Nestor, our produce vendor, was making his late afternoon deliveries to the restaurants, cook-shops, and *kapēleia* across the city and caught the glitter of the fibula against the pavement. At the very least, I hoped the fibula could save Binyamin's life too.

My cheeks softened as the warmth of knowing I'd get it back flooded through me.

"But you'll have something coming to you after your final bout?" I meant it as a statement, but it came out like a question.

"Not much there either. I've already borrowed against my purse and the bonus for winning the match."

He must have noticed me grip the edge of the desk, because he reached out to pat my arm.

"Don't worry, Sis, I'm sure I'll win."

I uttered a brief, noncommittal hum, but at that point, right or wrong, I was more concerned about his profligate spending than the possibility he'd lose.

"Anyway," he continued, "I had no choice. I had to pay for the few things Tychon and I would need for our voyage. The *ludus* pays for only the cheapest accommodations, deck passage. That's where you sleep in your own small tent on the deck with everybody else." He tapped his lip with the tip of his index finger to give the rest of that memory time to surface. "Oh yeah, and the *ludus* provides the food: beans, dried fruit, and barley, if you call that food. They expect us to cook all that into a *sagina* for ourselves. That's the stew they fed us, like the slop you feed livestock, gives you a lot of gas but reduces bleeding. Supposed to, anyway. Even so, can you imagine me cooking?"

He flashed me an indulgent half-smile. "The other deck passengers at least had their slaves to cook for them. But look, that's ancient history," he said, his chin thrust forward, his lips parting with excitement. "What I really need is a down payment to purchase the property and a mortgage to rebuild its campus. I figured on my inheritance from Papa for the down payment and a mortgage from you and Amram for the rest."

I took a deep breath, but I didn't have to look into the eyes of the asp.

"Okay, let's talk about the down payment. When you left, you expressly forsook your inheritance. Nevertheless, Papa established an account at our branch of the Bank of Gabinius with what would have been your half of his estate and regularly donated a portion of the balance to the Great Synagogue for the congregation to pray for you. What's more, his will stipulated that upon his death, the remainder would go directly to the Synagogue to continue their prayers for your safety and when the time came, to pray in perpetuity for your soul. So you see, Binny, he did love you."

"What?" His eyes widened as he froze into a stunned silence.

The only sound was the low-pitched trill of the warbler in the courtyard.

Binyamin's lips shaped words, but none came out.

Until he exploded.

"By Jupiter, that's the most outrageous thing I've ever heard. I can't believe he squandered my money that way. Except I can. Like I told you, he never supported my dreams. Couldn't he have believed in me, okay, if not as a son then at least as an athlete?"

Pulling at his hair, he rocked back and forth before recovering that Roman self-control he prided himself on.

His hands were trembling, but sitting back, he clasped them to hide the tremor.

So I dropped my eyes to the lacework the western sun was sketching on the floor as it peeked through the foliage in the courtyard. Once Binyamin released a sigh, I stole a glimpse and saw he'd unclenched his jaw and with his head tilted, was gently stroking his chin.

"Well," he said with a dismissive flip of his hand, "I'll just have to carry a bigger mortgage. You and Amram have the money."

"But, Binny, you have no assets to guarantee the loan. I can't ask Amram to finance a dream. We don't even know whether you could meet the payments let alone whether we should invest in what for us would be a shadowy enterprise."

"A shadowy enterprise! What's the matter with you? Have you forgotten? I'm your brother, your *twin* brother."

"Please, Binny, don't shout. You're disturbing the household."

He slapped a hand on the desk, stood, and leaned into me, crowding me with his stench, a combination of sour sweat, stale urine, and last night's vomit. "The household? Don't talk to me about this household," he shrieked. "This is my household too."

"Actually, Binny, it's not. Once you left, you were entitled to only the pearls and your half of the rest of our mother's jewelry. Papa didn't have to give you the jewelry you know, but he did so out of a sense of fairness to you."

Our parents' marriage contract specified that in accord with our tradition, if our mother predeceased our father, then their eldest son would inherit her dowry. Having lost their shipping business to piracy, our grandparents could provide her with only that single strand of Alexandrian pearls.

"You see, Binny, he really did love you. He just didn't know how to show it."

"Well, how about that! He just didn't know how to show it!" With his knuckles on his hips, he mimicked me in a tone thick with sarcasm. "And are you gonna blame me for that too?" He rolled his eyes, something I remembered Noah doing.

After an uncomfortable silence, his shoulders slumped forward. "Look, I knew I'd never get any help from our loving father, but now I see I'll never get any from you either. I used to think we were friends, that you were my soul mate, my co-conspirator. After all, we both killed our mother, right?" His voice quivered, but he steadied it with a long breath.

Then his eyes darted about the room as if scanning a cluttered attic for a treasured memento.

"Remember how we used to play together? All that kid stuff, challenging each other to stand on our heads, shinny up a tree, mount the sphinxes by the Gymnasium, and rush the mule carts for a ride to the beach? You name it, we did it. The only thing you couldn't do was somersault over the carts' tailgates. I'll never forget when you landed on that pile of dung."

For a moment, it looked like he might smile. His voice had risen a little, but then it quieted to a vicious but controlled anger. "I thought when you hired that fancy litter and accompanied me to the pier, or when you visited me in my cell after my win in Caesarea, or when you sent me letters begging me to come home, I thought, well, all that time I thought you wanted us to be together again, you know, like before. But I was wrong. You're just like Papa: judgmental, opinionated, and pigheaded. Remember what I used to say? That he acts like he's doing what's best for us, but he's just engineering what's best for himself. Well, the joke's on me. I waited till he was dead to come home only to find he's still here."

Binyamin singed me with his words. And nailed me with his stare.

Contempt flared in his eyes, and half-moons darkened his armpits.

Then he hawked a gout of phlegm and spewed it at my feet before stalking out and slamming the doors closed.

I pressed the heels of my palms against my temples, but I knew only another dose of mandrake could staunch this headache. So I called again for Calisto.

# Chapter 7

*Tuesday Afternoon, September 28th*:

The afternoon was usually hot for late September so Aunt Hannah and I sat in the atrium facing the pool, either sipping our ginger tea or resting the glasses beside us on the bench, our conversation drifting from food to fashions, or maybe the other way around. I really wanted to discuss Binyamin's request for a loan with her, but I didn't want to risk being overheard.

Given the heat of the day and the scant rainfall since May, Solon and Orestes were trudging in and out, fetching water from the well to keep the pool filled and the air circulating.

So I called for Adonia to help Aunt Hannah to my

sitting room, the sun having deserted my suite hours ago in favor of the western side of our house.

Adonia, buxom and white-haired with a rosy face studded with widely-spaced teeth, padded into the atrium. Once I got up, she wedged her shoulder under my aunt's arm and lifted her to a wobbly stance. Then, shifting their weight and leaning into one another with Adonia stooping slightly, they listed with an ursine heaviness down the corridor to our family's private suites.

Calisto had kept my windows and drapes closed against the morning sun so a dry, quiet smell, reminiscent of the chambers in the Great Library, greeted us. The room was awash in an imperfect darkness with pinpricks of light piercing the silk panels to cast faint stripes of color and shadow across the room.

Adonia arranged my aunt in the center of the sofa, thumping a few throw pillows, and cushioning her with them. Then she cut across the shadows to light the terracotta oil lamp on the marble top of my writing table while I took one of the occasional chairs and gave my aunt a few moments to spread out her arms and recognize her surroundings.

I asked Adonia to bring us some fresh tea. While waiting, we sat in a comfortable silence enjoying the delicate spice of the vanilla-scented lamp oil and the calm of our own long, even breaths.

Adonia returned with a silver tray carrying fresh glasses of tea, this time mint-flavored, and a gold-leaf platter fitted with cut glass bowls brimming with pitted dates, shelled pistachio nuts, and sesame cakes.

Placing the bowls along with the tea on the cedar table between Aunt Hannah and me, she unfurled an Indian cotton napkin for each of us and took my aunt's hand to show her where everything was. I waited until the door shut and the rhythmic echo of Adonia's feet followed her back toward the atrium.

"Miriam, you must have something on your mind."

"Oh, you know me too well, Auntie. In fact, I do. It's about Binyamin."

My Aunt shifted the pillows to turn toward me and reached for a date, while I told her about Binyamin's visit, not about his skill at aiming phlegm—I didn't mention that at all—but about his plan to buy, rebuild, and manage the *ludus* here.

"Well, I know how sordid that business is, something your father would have reprehended, but your father's not here, your brother is, and he's never shown an interest in anything else. So, my question is does he have the resources?"

"If you mean the connections, I believe the answer is yes. But if you mean the money, then the answer is no, not even a down payment. He's broke."

"Well, that settles it, doesn't it?"

She nibbled on the end of the date and then wiped her mouth and hands on the napkin while I took a long sip of the already tepid tea.

My glass made a clang when I set it back down on the table. “That’s just it, Auntie. He assumed Amram and I would finance him, the down payment as well as the mortgage. I told him no, that he needed to demonstrate he could carry the loan, and besides that, Amram and I would consider the enterprise too seedy. No, I said ‘too shadowy.’ Something like that. I suppose I could have been more tactful. I should have said we’re used to investing in—I don’t know—more conventional businesses. Anyhow, he was highly insulted, and I regret that. But that evening, I sat down with Papa’s abacus and realized I could finance the entire project myself, without involving Amram at all. So I began to wonder whether I’d been too hasty. So, what do you think, Auntie? Did I do the right thing?”

I scooped up a handful of pistachio nuts in preparation for her answer.

“Look, you know I don’t have a head for business. Music yes, business no, but still I’d say you did the right thing, except, as you said, you could have been more tactful. Let’s face it. Binyamin came to you without a business plan, and he’s had no experience sticking to a budget.”

*An understatement if I ever heard one.*

“You could, though, show him how to develop one.”

I’d been munching on the nuts so I took another, longer sip of tea to wash them down and get my voice back. “Okay. I could do that. Just yesterday afternoon, I met with a prospective client in the agora, at a *kapēleion*, the one with the pastries we like. He's a perfume maker from Judea who'd like to establish a perfumery here. I could show Binyamin his plan so he'd know what it's supposed to look like." I plucked a stray crumb of a pistachio nut off the table and put it in my mouth while Aunt Hannah bent her face toward her glass of tea. "There's another problem though, aside from the money. I'm concerned about underwriting a business that exploits human misery, like what I saw in Caesarea. Seeing Binyamin in a cage like that was bad enough, but at least he's been valued for his skill."

Aunt Hannah listened while she drank from her glass. "Well, how about giving him, yes, giving him—after all, you'll never have another brother—giving him the down payment if he can interest another investor. That way you're not involved, but you're starting him off with some money and a plan."

"You know, Auntie, that's why I appreciate your advice so much—"

"But wait, Miriam. I'm a little surprised. You said you met with a prospective client yesterday afternoon, and I know you're so exacting about details. How could you have been in the agora when you were here in the house with Kastor?"

"With Kastor? Yesterday afternoon? You've got to be kidding! You know he's not welcome here. Why, of all people, would you think he was here?"

"Because I heard him."

"Are you sure?"

"Yes, I recognized him from years ago, his awkward gait. I was in the library with Adonia arranging the roses she cut for me when I heard him dragging that clumsy foot of his across the atrium and into your study. I'm sure of it. So I figured you were with him."

"No, and I can't imagine what he was doing here."

But I was going to find out, and, when I did, I knew I wouldn't like it, not one bit.

# Chapter 8

*Wednesday Afternoon, September 29th*:

I called through the open doors of my study. "Minta, are you there? Someone's coming up the front steps. Please see whether it's Mr. Binyamin."

I was at my desk by early afternoon, finally identifying this universe as mine, realizing I had to assume ownership or I'd never convince Binyamin I was head of this household. Poring over the Judean's proposal, the beads of my abacus spinning and clicking in their marble grooves, I wanted to show the format to Binyamin. But these days, he was rarely around. He'd go out late in the afternoon, return around dawn, sometimes later, and hibernate in his suite until well past noon.

The weather was still unseasonable, the heat lingering like an unwelcome guest, but I had to draft a response for the perfume maker. So I opened all the doors hoping to enjoy one last breath from the Etesians, those seasonal, northwesterly winds that temper our summer sun. But no, instead of rustling the boxwood hedges, tunneling through the peristyle, and billowing the drapes, the air remained lifeless, searing the membranes of my nostrils and burning my lungs with plumes of fire.

Minta appeared, her eyes keen, her milk-white face poised to please.

"Mr. Binyamin's not up yet, Miss Miriam, but Mr. ben Israel is here." Her high, warble melted in the air. Then her eyebrows lifted like those of a schoolgirl with a question.

"Yes Minta, invite him in, and please bring us some tea."

She nodded him toward my study and then almost collided with him as she scampered away to fetch the tea.

"Come in, Gershon. Please," I said as my arm waved his weary body and careworn face through the doors. "It's been a few days. I thought you'd forgotten all about me," I teased, tilting my head and pinching my face into a mock pout. Actually, I just assumed he'd given up on coaxing us to liquidate our Judean holdings.

But I was wrong.

He told me Amram had readily agreed, and after a frantic search Monday that sent them rummaging through the entire house, they finally found the token, a square lead *tessera*, in of all places, a basket of aniconic coins that Amram had been keeping under his sleeping couch as a souvenir of his boyhood pilgrimage to Jerusalem.

"So Orestes and I went to the Public Records Office yesterday. And that's why I'm here. Not about your investments, something more urgent. Honestly, Miriam, I feel as if the Fates are thwarting my every good intention," he said, his voice concussive enough to whisk the lazy air.

No one had to tell me Gershon was troubled. Gloom floated on the wings of his emerald green, silk cloak. If anything, his face was more deeply corrugated than even on Sunday, the grooves set like hardened wax.

"So Orestes and I went to the Public Records Office. Wait. Didn't I already tell you that?" His eyes widened in a moment of confusion. "Well, I made two lists of the documents in his box, one for you and one for Amram, right in front of the underfed jackal you mentioned."

He reached inside his cloak, took out a roll of papyrus tucked inside his sash, unfurled it, his fingers trembling like a pigeon's wings, and placed it before me.

"When I showed it to Amram, he looked it over and gaped. Instead of being pleased, even grateful, he got so upset, insisting his will should have also been in the box. 'Where's my will?' he shrieked, his eyes accusing me as if I were a street swindler instead of his life-long friend!"

"Hush, Gershon," I said, patting the desk. His face

was glazed with perspiration, and my ears were screaming with pain.

"Praise the Lord," he said, dropping his voice, albeit temporarily, "at least Orestes was there to confirm that the will was missing before we opened the box."

At that moment Minta bustled in with the tea, fortunately chamomile. She must have heard Gershon's outrage ripping through the house.

She poured the tea, fussing with the glasses, fluttering the napkins, and then stood at Gershon's elbow to entice him to take a sip. Instead he dismissed her with a flick of his hand. So she just shrugged and whirled out the door, this time almost colliding with Binyamin, who was charging down the hall, his face smeared with stubble, the leather strips of his unlaced sandals whipping the air and smacking the floor. He bolted out the door but not before shooting me a malignant look that ended with his upper lip curled. I reached for the tea to wash down the bitterness. Draining the glass like a desert nomad, I stared at the dregs until Gershon broke into my half-formed thoughts.

"I didn't report the loss to you yesterday because I hoped that after a thorough search of his study, Amram and I would find the will and I'd be redeemed in his eyes. So we spent the rest of the day scouring every inch, ransacking every cabinet, and unrolling every scroll on all those shelves, even the ones furred with dust that climbed clear to the ceiling. This morning, we finished by riffling through the sheets of papyrus that shingle his floor. Nothing. As if it never existed.

"My only hope, Miriam, is that you might have it."

"No, Gershon, I don't." And this time, I meant it. "But, if it's lost, we can make another. It will take some time, but—"

He leaned forward, cupping his ears.

"I said it will take some time, but—"

"But that's just it. We don't have time. When I saw Amram this morning, he was flushed with fever and gasping for air. I tell you Death was staring him in the face. Leo immediately went for the physician, who examined Amram's tongue and then wrung his hands. A few grave sighs later, he gave Amram some mandrake to reduce his fever and began the bloodletting to clear his ch—"

"But what did the physician say?"

"He said what they all say, that either Amram will kill the disease or the disease will kill him."

"Dear Lord, why didn't you tell me he's sick?" I cried, wheeling out of my chair, pumping my fists like a madwoman. "And the treatment is all wrong! Amram needs his blood! You see how pale he's been!"

"Egad, you're right."

I squeezed my arms around my chest and breathed deeply to regain my composure, but the taste of fear remained on my lips.

"Let Orestes and Solon take you back right away.

Tell the physician to stop the bloodletting and have him tie ligatures instead—not too tightly—around Amram's arms and legs, near his shoulders and just below the groin, to trap the blood in his limbs and keep it from flooding his chest. Then send Taharqa or Rho to Aspasia's for some garlic to ease his breathing."

*The garlic will also improve his circulation, as long as he's not sensitive to onions or ginger*, I thought, reviewing the cautions in *De Medicina* that I'd studied with Hector.

"In the meantime, I'll pack up some willow. It'll reduce the fever more gently than mandrake and ease any distress. But in case his suffering becomes severe or he begins to vomit, get some cannabis as well. Do that, and I'll come over as soon as I can."

Gershon was already on his feet when I called to Minta.

"Come right away! Get Orestes and Solon to bring the chair out front for Mr. ben Israel. Then ask the cook to wrap up a bundle of willow. And have Calisto bring me my *calcei* and himation. And hurry. Please."

~

Squinting against the mica-flecked cobbles, I panted the few blocks to Amram's house, overtaking each mansion, its familiar columns, arches, and balconies glittering in the late afternoon sun. The branches of plane trees reached out to urge me on while the oven of air parched my lips and blistered the inside of my mouth. Grasshoppers and lizards, sparrows and larks fled from me as I thundered through the dust clutching the bundle of willow branches in one hand and taming the skirt of my tunic with the other.

Once I neared the box hedge, I saw Gershon's haggard face framed in the grid-covered porter's hole, his frown lines etched more deeply than even earlier this afternoon. As soon as he ushered me in and the great front door clanged shut, I could see that a forward stoop and wobbly knees had replaced his perfect posture.

"The physician left a while ago, a triangular-faced fellow with idiot eyes and a head too large for his neck. Do you know him?" I started to nod, but Gershon didn't wait for my answer. "He removed the ligatures but showed Leo how to tie them when the cough returns. He didn't say *if*, he said *when* the cough returns. And he said to keep the mandrake handy, that the fever is bound to spike."

Dread flickered in Gershon's eyes as he gripped my wrist like a vice.

We stood there blinking at each other until I remembered why I'd come.

"Give this willow to the cook so she can make an extract," I said, handing him the bundle, but his thoughts had yet to coil back from their cavernous place.

"Thankfully, he's sleeping now," he mumbled,

"maybe visiting Noah, or his Leah and their daughters, all of them at His side so many years now."

"But I must see him now," I said, dragging Gershon back from that distant landscape.

He jerked his head and rubbed the back of his neck. "Then prepare yourself. I'll lead the way," he said, taking the bundle but only to toss it onto the bench.

As soon as we left the eucalyptus-scented atrium, the acrid breath of Amram's sickness, a pungent mixture of flatulence, soiled linens, and dried blood, assailed my nostrils. The stench become more insistent with each tiptoe along the palatial corridor, past silk drapes swagged to reveal room after room of massive, highly varnished furniture, some walls veneered in marble, others frescoed with murals of trees, birds, and mythical animals.

Surrounded by a battery of squat tables, some rosewood, others mahogany and teak, each jammed with herbs and unguents, vials and flasks, ligatures and sweat-drenched towels, Amram looked smaller than ever on his sleeping couch, like a skin-draped skeleton, his teeth too big for his face. His ancient hands were translucent as they poked out from the coverlet, his knuckles as iridescent as a string of pearls. His face was flecked with fever and his lips caked with dried blood, but his breathing, though shallow, was regular.

Poor, poor Amram. So sick. And Gershon so worried. I didn't have the heart to tell him that replacing the will could take a long time. Oh, I remembered the terms. They were fairly simple. Years ago, shortly after Noah died, Amram made me his principal heir. But I'd just taken his seal ring to Judah's shop for repair. The gold had worn so thin that when I last used it, the hoop split at the bottom and broke off from the shoulders of the ring.

And gold was so scarce. Judah said he'd have to send to Spain for the ingots, that I'd have to be patient if he could get the gold at all, that pirates continue to target the shipments even when they're carried by military transport. To think I had the ring in my study all these years, but when I positively needed it, it was out of reach. *Maybe*, I thought, *Judah hasn't started working on it yet, and somehow I can grasp just the shoulders of the ring around the signet to seal Amram's new will.* Like Gershon, I began to feel as if the Fates were plotting against us.

But more to the point, how could the will have disappeared? I myself had secured it in Amram's box, and he and I were the only ones with the token. So what could have happened to it?

# Chapter 9

*Thursday Morning, September 30th*:

"No, not this one," I bleated, pitching the green tunic toward my sitting room sofa, missing the toss and watching the fabric pool on the floor. The second tunic I'd tried on that morning and I was running out of options. "Please, one more, the white one with the border print."

"That's the only one left, Miss Miriam," said Minta between nibbles on her upper lip.

Calisto and Minta had taken extra care with my grooming that morning, First they washed me, cut my nails, and combed jasmine oil through my long chestnut hair to add softness and luster as well as to calm my spirits with its fragrance. I was always anxious before seeing Judah.

Next Minta rubbed my face with a pumice stone while Calisto plaited my hair into four braids, and pulled them back into a bun, which she held in place with sapphire-tipped pins and a gold-threaded net. After that, Calisto set ringlets at my temples. Holding the *calamistrum* by its wooden handle, her lips pressed in concentration, she heated the metal rod in a brazier before winding the locks around it.

Minta must have flashed her a signal because Calisto's features momentarily sharpened. And then when Minta went to fetch the white tunic and picked a deep blue sash to gird my waist, Calisto had already returned with my lapis lazuli necklace and the set of matching stones for my ears, gifts from my father. He used to say they captured the blue of my eyes and made them luminous.

Almost ready, I worked my feet into a pair of ankle-high boots and spun around so they could check the drape of the fabric. Then I calmed the skirt so they could approve the height of the border print. A tug here and there and I was in compliance with Roman fashion. Reaching into my cosmetic box and bringing out a vial of oil of red ochre, Calisto brushed a drop on my lips, saying "You look so pale today, Miss Miriam."

Finally, Minta wrapped me in my himation and fastened it at my shoulder with a gold brooch.

My eyes misted when I realized I'd soon be wearing my mother's fibula again. But once more, I'd be wrong. Terribly wrong.

ʚɞʚɞ

By the time I reached the Great Synagogue, the congestion on the Canopic Way had forced me to limit the length of my strides, while the caravans and chariots, wagons and oxcarts, sedan chairs and litters each cast a shifting shadow on the sun-warmed pavement. As I headed toward the agora and Judah's shop, the smell of tethered animals and unwashed bodies combined with the brine of the sea, the odor of beached algae, the aroma of fresh pastries, and the reek of urine collecting in the earthenware bowls at every fuller's gate.

And then a breeze off Lake Mareotis sifted through my himation, and feathering my nose with the fragrance of the dwarf pines in the Park of Pan, awakened my memories of Judah. After seeing him, I'd often stroll along the pine-shaded walkways dedicated to this playful god and spiral around the fir-cone shaped hill to the summit. There I'd look out at the splendid city encircling me, wishing my own future could press beyond its walls as Alexandria's sprawl had pressed beyond hers.

And so my mind slipped back to my sixteenth year when, in response to Papa's request that I begin collecting our mortgagers' payments, I first walked into

Judah's shop. How could I ever forget that morning? How the oil lamps brushed his face with light and splashed his pearly shadow across the white tile floor. How the new day's air mingled with his own sandalwood fragrance. When he raised his lids to look at me, his eyes widening and his pupils dilating, I felt as if he'd touched me, and a flutter deep inside me, like an ache, raw but exquisite, earthy but mystical, stirred me to life.

Suddenly, love was no longer an abstraction. From that moment on, every detail of his face and physique would be etched in my memory, from his high-bridged nose, rugged cleft chin, glossy black curls, and luminous green eyes to his well-chiseled muscles, broad shoulders, narrow waist, and calloused hands. Nothing would matter—not my reputation, my betrothal to Noah, nor my standing as a Roman citizen—until I could once again fill my eyes with the sight of him, my ears with the sound of him, and my lungs with the scent of him. And from then on, I would long for him, both shyly and eagerly, passionately and tenderly.

As the years passed, I came to know every inflection of his voice and every sparkle in his eyes, but still I'd be forbidden to love him. Without Roman citizenship or membership in any other privileged class, he had no redress in the Roman courts and no immunity from the complex array of Roman taxes, especially the *laographia* or poll tax, a tax on all accountable males between the ages of fourteen and sixty, slaves included. Consequently, a single misfortune could mire him in poverty or worse yet, plunge him into slavery. Then the tax collector would drag him off to the slave exchange where he'd stand in chains naked on a platform so perspective purchasers could inspect him while pockets of dealers lounged on benches nattering along the sidelines.

And if that wasn't enough to fuel my father's opposition, Judah was a bastard, the illegitimate son of an orphaned woman too poor to provide a dowry and therefore ineligible to marry. And so, when we ventured beyond the scrim to the spartan room in the rear of his shop that was his home and, in a single careless moment I fell into his arms, he warned me. "I'm no good for you. You were meant for a life I cannot give you. You need to go home now before you'd have to bear on your wedding night the stigma of this afternoon and the invectives that were hurled at my mother and me."

When I'd see him on the calends to collect his mortgage payment, and more often when I could conjure up a pretext, which I became highly skilled at doing, he'd speak to me about his work, his dreams, and his interest in alchemy. He even introduced me to the League of Alchemists and lent me its scrolls, one in particular with the secret recipe for perfecting copper into gold that he'd been developing with Saul, his mentor. Judah wanted me to understand their work, and so we'd spend hours together, our conversations meandering like the tributaries of the Nile, our voices melting together, the pitch intimate, the flow seamless. But never would I know him as a bride knows her groom, not his body and not his heart.

Breathless with desire as I fantasized about lying next to him on tousled sheets, I was so engrossed in re-living that dream-like stage of our relationship that I hardly remembered clipping past the Way's statues and temples, barrows and booths, colonnades and arcades until I was roused by a rush of pigeons as I turned north onto the Street of the Soma. Once I caught sight of its sun-bleached rooftops angling toward the agora like a row of broken teeth, my thoughts snapped back to Amram's ring.

And so, despite the welcomed coolness of that late-September morning, by the time I reached the agora, my underarms were sticky with dread. Jostled by shoppers through the crush of commerce, the clamor of craftsmen, and the harangue of hucksters, I nudged my way around the moneychangers' tables and the other portable businesses that clog the agora until I found myself at Judah's *stoa*, one of the long, low porticoed buildings that face the central plaza. Feigning an interest in the wares of a tinker's stall to check my appearance in the shine of his pots, I then dawdled for some moments behind a stack of Oriental carpets to brush spangles of dust from my himation, pinch color into my cheeks, and calm the hammer in my chest. What if I couldn't get Amram's ring back soon enough?

ꩰꩰ

Seated on a stool facing the entrance, arched over his workbench, examining a light-orange carnelian through a glass globe of water, Judah raised his thick lashes when I entered his shop on a gust of courage.

"Miriam! I didn't expect to see you today," he said after a double take.

Except for bringing him Amram's ring, which I'd done the day before Binyamin came home, I'd hardly seen him since his return from Caesarea almost three years ago. We'd exchange cordial greetings in the Great Synagogue on the Holy Days, but the rest of my days unrolled without him. He'd lost interest in the League after his mentor died, and he'd satisfied his mortgage with Papa long before he returned to Alexandria. So we no longer had a reason to see each other. Besides, everyone knew he was busier than ever with commissions from not just Alexandria and the upcountry towns along the Nile but the Holy Land and even as far away as Tyre.

At least that was what I told myself.

His new-found prosperity hadn't changed him, though. He continued to live the simple life his mother taught him to value since she died years before Miriam met Judah. His home was still the Spartan room behind the scrim, and he wore the same coarse, gray workingman's tunic, a *colobium*, short-sleeved, cut above the knee, and belted at the waist.

I watched the fabric tighten across his chest and spill over his thighs as he rose to greet me.

"I'm sorry, Miriam, but I told you Amram's ring would take a while," he said, his brows furrowed in perplexity.

*What? You think I don't know that?*

I screamed the words at him.

But only in my mind.

Instead I pinched my lips and grabbed a stool along his display counter to support my liquid knees. Signet rings, each with an intaglioed stone, were artfully arranged in one showcase after another along with bronze and brass cuff bracelets; pendants, charms, and amulets worked in silver or gold; cameos carved in glass or hardstone—onyx or agate—and brooches with complex mosaic designs set in malachite; each the work of a master craftsman in his prime.

"The ring, Miriam."

"Hmmm?"

"I asked you whether you're here for Amram's ring?"

That's Judah getting right to the point. Not "Hello, how are you?" or "You look lovely this morning." Nothing like that.

"Yes, I'm here about the ring, but not because I expect it to be ready. I knew it couldn't be. But I need it. Badly. Amram is ill, maybe dying, and I need to help him draft a new will without delay."

"You know, I've already taken the ring apart to reuse the remaining gold. I told you we'd have to wait for—"

"I know, I know," I said, my voice more shrill than I intended. "But look, isn't there any way I could get just the stone back? Couldn't you somehow fashion a way for me to grasp it so I could authenticate the new will?"

Judah funneled his lips and then nodded slowly.

"Yes, of course, we could do that. I could mount the stone, temporarily perhaps, in a bronze or iron set—"

"Oh, Judah, how soon? I'm worried about so many things, especially about Amram, whether he'll recover and how his will disappeared in the first place. And if there's a connection between the two events. Oh dear Lord, Amram could be in great danger. And then there's Gershon, the uprisings and mounting economic crisis in Judea, the collapse of his business.

"And, of course, Binyamin and that murderer he brought back from Capua, a dangerous man if I ever saw one, and I don't mean just in the arena. But that's another story. I told you he was coming home, didn't I? Binyamin, I mean. But I didn't know, I just never imagined—how could I?—that he'd make life so difficult, that he'd challenge—"

I tried to slow myself down, to control myself, but the words kept pouring out uncensored and unchecked until they flooded the entire shop.

"Well, if you need it that badly, I can have it for you right away." He raked his hands through his hair. "Come by tomorrow afternoon, and you'll have it before Shabbat."

"Oh, Judah, thank you." I whispered, closing my eyes, feeling the relief melt into my shoulders, only to pray the whole way home that tomorrow wouldn't be too late.

# CHAPTER 10

*Friday Afternoon, October 1st*:

"Miss Miriam, you forgot this!" Minta was running toward me waving my shopping satchel as I tripped down our side street in my rush to pick up Amram's seal ring before Shabbat.

I shook my head in frustration. Hours past midday, so late to be starting out, the crowds already thinning, the *balneae* emptying, peddlers packing up their wares, shopkeepers closing their stalls, and street vendors lowering their canopies, all energies focused on making it home before sundown.

I'd borne the weight of that morning, stretching out my routine to fill the slowly unfolding hours before I could sensibly leave for Judah's. I certainly didn't want to arrive early, to wait around wrestling with each embarrassing silence, seeding conversations about the weather and the price of beans, every second taking hours to limp along.

Besides, I was embarrassed. I'd burst in the day before, prevailed on him to drop everything, and then, when he agreed, I showed him my gratitude by punishing his ears with a babble of woes. But how could I send Minta or Calisto in my place? In spite of my foolish behavior, I still wanted to see Judah, to inhale his sandalwood scent and add another image of him to my treasured collection so I could ignite a fresh fantasy in the darkness of my *cubiculum*. Would the time ever come when I'd finish the day with more than just the fantasy of his embrace?

And where had the afternoon gone? My last task had been to check that the oil lamps were full so they'd burn straight through Shabbat. I'd finished that, had gotten dressed for the agora, and was checking my reflection in the silver-skinned surface of the atrium's pool when Solon told me the winch for drawing water from our well had jammed.

"Oh, no," I said, that news being only the first sign that my getting away wasn't going to be so easy.

"Miss Miriam, do you want me to take it apart now or wait till after Shabbat?"

Knowing better than to have Solon take anything

apart, let alone expect him to put it back together quickly or otherwise, but needing the water drawn before Shabbat, I asked him to find Orestes. Orestes could fix anything, probably better than even Hero. But where was my favorite handyman? Was he back yet from picking up the cook's produce order at the local plaza?

More distractions: Binyamin calling for breakfast when the cook was busy preparing tomorrow's grilled lamb, and then Minta, poor thing, trying to slice a few apricots to serve him with some yogurt but cutting herself in the process; too many other interruptions; the afternoon gathering speed; spinning out of control; pulling me in a million directions.

I could have saved time by having Solon and Orestes take me in the chair. By then, Orestes had been back for more than an hour, enough time to have fixed the winch and shaved Binyamin. But I didn't want them to see the longing stamped on my face when I was about to see Judah and worse yet, to pity me for still being single at twenty-seven. And so with that one additional delay for the satchel, I left for the agora later than planned.

ɞɞ

The heavy oak shutters were open, but by then, Judah had locked the wrought iron grille across the entrance to his shop. So I stood at the threshold bathed in a shaft of late-afternoon light, calling to him through the lattice, managing only a husky whisper. I was still gulping air from my sprint through the nearly deserted Street of the Soma, the last few blocks in a panic imagining he'd already begun his Shabbat preparations.

But no. He was standing by his workbench wiping down its surface with vinegar while picking up the metal scraps to store in an earthenware *cantharus*, the two-handled drinking cup he uses for that purpose. His brow was furrowed as if he was contemplating the riddle of the Sphinx, but when he raised his chin, his forehead smoothed.

"Miriam, is that you?" He strode toward the grille along the way grabbing the long wooden key that hung from a hook near the display counter. "You're so late. I'd given up on you," he said while unlocking the grille and pushing it open a few feet.

"Oh, Jud—much—before—leave." I said between gasps as I stepped inside on the long, shallow puddle that was my shadow. "So much to do before I could leave. Look, I'm really sorry for delaying you."

"No problem. I still have to sweep up. But come see the ring," he said, walking back to his workbench, the back of his head still a thicket of curls despite his thirty-five years. His movements were so natural, so fluid, so confident that the air graciously yielded to him.

"I set the stone in bronze," he said turning to face me, "but if you decide later you want it mounted in gold, I can do that as soon as we get the ingots."

*Another chance to see him.*

"I'm so relieved," I said, thanking him, grateful for the calm seeping into my bones as I examined the green oval agate, Amram's name inscribed in Hebrew across its face, the stone in a bezel setting, the shoulders and hoop of the ring shiny and substantial. And then, feeling the burn of an adolescent blush, I added but in a smaller voice, in itself an apology, "Please excuse me for burdening you with my troubles yesterday. Once I got started, I couldn't seem to stop."

"I was glad to set the stone for you," he said, his eyes alighting on mine before fleeing to a corner of the ceiling. "And for Amram. Besides, I could tell you were upset. About a few things."

I squeezed my eyes shut and compressed my lips while deciding whether to confide in him about Binyamin.

"Maybe you've heard. Binyamin came back to Alexandria to fight his last bout. Once he's discharged, he wants to buy the *ludus* here."

"Well, given his experience—"

"But Judah, he wants me of all people to finance it. And I can't. I just can't. I saw more than I could stand of that life in Caesarea."

Judah nodded. He'd also been at those games in Caesarea. We'd sat at opposite ends of the Procurator's *tribunal* as guests of Judah's brother, whom Alexander was honoring for crafting the medallions for the victors.

But Judah never recognized Binyamin, and I was too ashamed to tell him that the *retiarius* named Agrippa Fortitudo was my very own brother.

"I dread attending Binyamin's bout but not because I'm afraid he'll lose. He told me he'll have an untrained opponent, a *noxi*, you know, a criminal, not an *auctoratus*. Maybe it's the thought of another death on my brother's hands or that free from his contract, he'll remain in Alexandria for good. I don't know myself. All I know is the bout's not until Wednesday, and already I'm as nervous as if I were fighting in the arena myself."

"You know, if it'd make it any easier, I'll go with you," he said, fanning out his palms.

"Oh, no. I couldn't ask that." I said, answering quickly, waggling my head, taken aback by his offer. "Not on top of resetting Amram's stone."

But he just shrugged. "Of course I'll go with you. Didn't you try to help my brother? And Saul? You even bathed him on his death bed. Which reminds me, I have some things of his I want to give you. So sit down a minute while I wrap up the ring."

I placed my satchel on the floor, adjusted the folds in my himation, and sat on one of the stools fronting his display counter. Then, swiveling in the seat, I watched him buff the ring, put it in a silk, draw-string pouch, and tuck the pouch inside a linen sheath. My eyes clung to every part of him but remained on alert to shift their gaze if, feeling my stare, he looked my way.

"Here," he said, moving toward me, handing me the packet, and sitting down next to me. "Let me tell you about Saul's things. I've kept them only because they belonged to him: his flasks and crucibles, filters and funnels," Judah started to tick off the items on his fingers and then simply said, "all his equipment." He leaned back for a moment and half closed his eyes. "And his minerals: Vials of orpiment, sandarac, siderite, and cinnabar. Others too," he added, stroking his chin and pursing his lips. "I just can't remember them all."

A melancholy expression took over his face. "I did what I could in Caesarea to comfort his soul. When I came home though, I still didn't feel ready to get rid of his things. Besides, I didn't know what to do with them. But I knew I wanted to give them to someone who'd remember him and use them as he intended. That's why I want you to take them. Please."

"Judah, I'd love to and for the reasons you say. Saul was as a master craftsman and brilliant alchemist, a loving father as well as your mentor. I'll pray for His Grace to do good with them."

But then I glanced at my shadow, so thin, stretching onto the far wall of his shop. It was time to go. Oh, how I yearned to linger, once again to enter his sanctum behind the scrim. I remembered it from years ago as a place of gentle sunlight. Only the soft morning rays could touch the louvers of his single, east-facing window. And I remembered it as a simple place with only a sleeping couch; washstand, pitcher, and basin; table and chair; and the two raw pine shelves that held all else he owned. But Shabbat was bearing down. Already I'd have to race against the draining light to make it home early enough to dress and reach Amram's house in time to light his candles.

So I secured the ring in my satchel. Then, patting his hand as it rested on the counter and feeling his warmth inside me, I stood and smoothed my himation over my tunic.

"I'll be back soon," I said, my voice hoarse, yet my throat unable to swallow.

"Wait, Miriam," he said as he skirted around me toward the grille. "Let me hail a chair for you."

I followed him out to the street. Pushing his index fingers under the tip of his tongue, pulling his lips over his teeth, and sealing his mouth around his fingers, he gave out a commanding whistle, something Binyamin had taught me to do whenever we wanted to hitch a ride to the beach. A moment later, Judah was beckoning a pair of bearers that emerged from the livery stable.

With a barely perceptible nod from Judah, the lead bearer tucked me into the chair. Once the team found its stride loping southward, I yawed in the chair, chased by the sun's last light, my heart beating in time with their boots, and Judah's eyes watching over me until we turned the corner.

# Chapter 11

*Saturday (Shabbat) Afternoon, October 2nd*:

I'd been expecting a knock on the door that afternoon, but it still sent a frisson of fear down my spine. After all, it might have been Gershon with another installment of dreadful news. Unlikely on Shabbat, I know, but what if it was? What if more of Amram's documents had turned up missing? Or what if Amram had had a relapse? True, he was better last night, his mind more alert and his skin no longer flushed with fever, but these rallies are so often the Herald of Death.

To my relief, the caller was Phoebe, my intrepid scout, co-conspirator, and best friend, who protects my secrets and helps me right my wrongs. Beginning her life with our family as the day-old, Greek foundling wrapped in the soiled blanket my mother happened upon in the *Bruchium* quarter, Phoebe became more than our household slave, even more than our beloved servant. Five years my senior, she became the big sister who'd join me in my lessons with Hector. Later on, she became the unshakable optimist in my uncertain romance with Judah as well as the officious critic of my manners and dress.

I'd never forget when we were staying in that saggy-floored, attic *cella* in Caesarea and I was dressing to go with Judah to his brother's house for Shabbat dinner, my first opportunity to meet him. Posing like an artist with her head cocked, she insisted on choosing the tunic. "Forget the crimson," she said. "Too much color. You're not going to the theater, Miriam. You're going to someone's home."

Even then I knew better than to argue. And since her husband Bion set sail for Athens, she's become my regular Shabbat afternoon guest.

Upon crossing the threshold, she cut short our trills of mutual delight to open her arms, gather me to her pillowy bosom, and swallow me up in the folds of her body. I heard her sweet mewing and inhaled the warm lavender scent rising from her skin.

Then, as if stitched together, we swayed like a two-headed sailor rocking on deck with the swells until she arched her neck and we slowly broke apart, her dark, widely-spaced eyes backlit with devotion. Phoebe's hugs were the closest I'd ever come to a mother's embrace.

Looking her over, her hands locked in mine, I tried to square the still-surprising image of this prosperous matron with the one that persists in my mind's eye. Two years ago, in anticipation of her marriage to Bion, she agreed to her manumission so their children would be free. Until then I'd seen her in only the coarse gray woolen tunic that marked her status as a slave.

Bion, also a former slave but owned by the civil authorities, repaired scrolls in the workshop of the Great Library. Now he owns a thriving *bibliopōleion* in the agora, where he deals in rare classical manuscripts as well as the contemporary work of scholars like Thrasyllus of Mendes and engineers like our very own Hero. But his liveliest trade is in writing supplies: the ink, inkwells, bronze and reed pens, sharpening knives, and styli along with the sheets and scrolls of papyrus and parchment for the myriad of clerks, students, and scholars who populate our city.

So nowadays Phoebe dresses in a Chinese silk or Spanish linen *tunica interior* that along its lower edge sports an *instita*, a wide (and her case, deeply embroidered and voluminous) ornamental flounce. Atop that, she wears a *stola*, the married woman's traditional boxy outer garment, the hem of hers barely brushing the top of her *instita* so she can flaunt this latest Roman style. And, in keeping with her status as the wife of a successful shopkeeper, she adorns herself with necklaces, amulets, and pendants; a few snake bracelets; perhaps a brooch; and one or two massive rings, each studded with gems. That day, I noticed her ellipsoid hoop earrings made of spirally-twisted gold wires, clearly the work of Judah's hands.

But don't let her finery fool you. Every week she arrived bursting with gossip as if she'd been ladling soup in the public kitchens or eavesdropping outside the city's barber shops, whorehouses, and dice games.

"Phoebe, you look so glamorous!"

Her familiar giggle wafted through the atrium's peaceful Shabbat air.

"Come. We'll lunch upstairs." I turned toward the bench and lifted a tray with the crater of wine, a silver bowl of mint sauce, and an Oriental platter of the grilled lamb I'd cobbled together for our lunch. I'd carved the meat and spread the slices across layers of chopped olives, dandelion greens, and the pita the cook baked yesterday in anticipation of Shabbat. On Fridays, she bakes enough for both days.

Phoebe's *instita* swirled like froth as we climbed the stairs to the third-floor, Egyptian-style roof garden, our favorite place in years past to enjoy a summer breakfast of dates, goat cheese, and muffins flavored with coriander seeds. I couldn't wait to tell her about Judah, that I'd be seeing him again soon, maybe often, but as she was my guest, I gave her the opportunity to tell me her news first.

"So when will Bion be home?" I asked as I put the tray down on a wrought iron stand and placed the crater, bowl, and platter on the marble table.

Phoebe and I took seats across from each other on teak benches banked with cushions of cerulean and turquoise silk. Her squint lines relaxed in the amber-tinted shade of the roof garden's bleached linen canopy while the cityscape below us throbbed with light under a hard blue sky. Just as I began to ladle the wine into goblets and she'd finished smoothing her skirts, a drowsy breeze sifted through our hair, brushed the potted palms that screened us from our front and side streets, and tossed the heads of the peonies in their haphazardly arranged planters.

"His ship should arrive in a few weeks, certainly before the beginning of November," she answered while rearranging the tableware I'd set up earlier. "In fact, he could be leaving for home this very day." A glitter of excitement ignited her eyes.

We both knew no one can predict a ship's departure date. It depended on so many factors: the winds; the time of the month, never at the end; divinations from the pre-sail sacrifice; ominous dreams, especially of shipwrecks, storms, pirate attacks, wild boars, and owls or other night birds; and additional black portents like a sneeze on the gangway or a crow perched on the rigging.

"After all, the season's almost over so he's bound to be on one of the next cargo ships headed for Alexandria."

Phoebe lifted her chin, closed her eyes, and taking a deep breath of the peony-scented air, smiled at the world. After a while, she added, "Wouldn't it be funny if he sails on the *Orion*? Of course, he couldn't possibly have the accommodations we had."

Phoebe was referring to our trip to Caesarea, the one my father arranged for us on his cousin Samson's *corbita*, a wide sailing ship with a rounded, big-bellied hull for cargo. As special guests of Eli, Samson's son, we enjoyed the luxury of his deckhouse if not the pleasure of his company.

I took the moment to remember how crude I thought Eli was, although at this point, I see him as merely foolish in his clumsy attempts to impress me, perhaps even court me. But his conceit was as swollen as his belly which, draped with swags of fat, rolled over his pigskin girdle. He'd bellow and bluster about his business triumphs all the while oblivious to my squelched yawns. Now I can laugh, but at the time his boasting bored me, his sour belches revolted me, and more than that, his overtures embarrassed me.

"Well, why are you smiling, Miriam? Do you really think Bion might be sailing home on the *Orion*?"

"Could be, you know, if Eli was able to expand the trade routes of his father's shipping business. Remember, after he dropped us and Gershon off in Caesarea, he planned to sail on to Cyprus and Byzantium to do just that."

As I spooned the mint sauce over the lamb, Phoebe, exercising both her theatrical talent and elaborate imagination, began to recount our arrival in Caesarea and that first glimpse of the harbor. She must have commented on every tug lined up in the choppy sea outside the northern breakwater and each team of husky, sun-bronzed rowers. Even I recalled among the scores of grain ships the one with a latrine suspended beyond its sternpost, but I could hardly have pictured the rest of it.

"Miriam, I refuse to believe you don't remember its deck lined with all those tents—I tell you they were huge—and its tutelage, that gilded statue of Poseidon, trident and all, atop its poop deck." She cast up her eyes and sighed with exasperation. "Surely you remember its red topsail!"

I only remembered that needle-like ache for Judah and later, shading my eyes against a shaft of morning sun, searching the crowded promenade for that one face wreathed in curls.

Only after Phoebe described that stunning view of the Temple of Augustus and Roma, seeing "those colossal statues on their lofty platform beckoning me to find my true love in their city" did she take her first sip of wine.

Actually, I recalled our arrival differently, that she was resoundingly opposed to our looking up Bion, that I had to insist it was necessary to our mission. But that's what we do when we get together. We re-tell our stories and embroider them with fresh details and meanings.

"Well, that was quite a sight, wasn't it, Miriam?"

At that point, I wasn't sure which sight she had in mind, surely not the statues beckoning her, but I pinched my lips and nodded just the same.

"Well, I can't believe Bion's been away since May," Phoebe said, waggling her head. Her eyes drifted toward the sea and glazed over as if she was recalling his departure.

But then a stiff breeze flapped the sides of the canopy, splashing her with a shower of lemony light and splaying the wispy feathers of dark hair that played across her untroubled brow. Her concentration broken, she reached for and snatched the napkins before the breeze could claim them.

"May? That long? Really?" I asked while fishing out a stray dandelion leaf, ready to savor its bitterness.

Phoebe nodded. "His exit visa came through as soon as the director of the Great Library arranged passage for him."

*The advantage of an insider dealing with those haughty port officials.*

"So Bion was able to leave at the beginning of the sailing season and get there by July. The director sent him to expand the Library's collection of the Athenian comic poets as long as Bion could verify the editions as canonical. Of course, the director will easily earn back the Emperor's investment—plus, I'm sure, a little for himself—when his scribes make copies for the wealthy bibliophiles throughout the Empire.

Phoebe pulled off a hunk of pita and took a deep bite. I pulled off another, spread it with a slice of lamb and some chopped olives, put it on her plate, and waited for her to eat it.

While she brushed away the pita crumbs with the edge of her bejeweled hand, I peeled off a slice of lamb for myself, put it on my plate, cut it in half, and popping it in my mouth, relished the hearty flavor that burst across my tongue.

"Bion wants to buy at least one scroll to display in the shop. He said it would attract customers. And in a recent letter, he told me he'll also be bringing home a copy of Menander's *Dyskolos* because he was just like Sostratos who, according to the story, fell instantly in love with Knemon's daughter.

A life-loving smile began in Phoebe's eyes, spread to her lips, poked dimples in her cheeks, and then expanded into a shy giggle.

"But I have to say the time's been passing quickly. Most days I help out in the shop alongside Galen and Thoth."

They're the clerks Bion brought with him when he closed his shop in Caesarea.

"'Too much turmoil to run a business in Judea.' That's what Bion told me. 'Even Caesarea is vomiting blood.' Between the strikes and revolts, terrorism and banditry—" Phoebe punctuated each brand of strife with a wave of her spoon. "—assassinations and ambushes, he couldn't get the goods he needed, not even papyrus from the banks of the Jordan, never mind the silky sheets from here. 'Besides,' he said. 'No one has any money, certainly not the peasants pouring in through the city gates, worse off than ever having sold their land to pay their civil taxes.'

"It's so different here." Phoebe made a sweeping gesture with her arms as if to encompass the entire city. "All day, every day, snaking lines of customers, mostly regulars like the public slaves Bion used to know when he worked at the Library. But also tourists. You should see the beads on Galen's abacus fly when he calculates the cost of their purchases. Regardless of the currency, he's faster than even the moneychangers outside the shop."

Sometimes I wonder how my life might have been different had I simply plunked the rest of that slice of lamb in my mouth and we'd finished our lunch to the melody of chinking cutlery and tinkling glassware.

But I didn't.

Instead I asked about Kastor.

I have no idea why Kastor crossed my mind just then. Perhaps because Aunt Hannah mentioned she'd heard him in the house, although the more I thought about it, the more convinced I became that she had to have been mistaken. Or perhaps because Phoebe mentioned the slaves in the Public Records Office patronizing the shop. Not surprising. After all, time was when Bion had been a slave of the civil authorities too. So, why shouldn't Kastor be his customer?

"Well, is Kastor—"

Phoebe's spoon landed on the table with a clang. "Oh, you just reminded me!"

When she pushed her chair back and crossed her knees, I knew I was about to hear a new story.

Phoebe glanced left and right before lowering her voice to a whisper. "Kastor is dead, brutally murdered yesterday, beaten with some sort of club, although the authorities have yet to find the weapon."

Phoebe continued after a dramatic pause. "He died in his room at The Pegasus, a jagged cut at the back of his head."

I winced as if I too had been cut there.

"The Pegasus?" I asked in a barely audible squeak. "That shabby waterfront flophouse where Binyamin stayed until his ship sailed for Rome?" I didn't feel like mentioning I knew someone else who was staying there now. Why open another pair of parentheses?

"That very one."

"Why on Earth would he be there? He has—I mean had—a room in the *Bruchium* quarter, much closer to his work. He'd been there for years, ever since he left us."

"I don't know," she said with a shrug. "Ask Isis. All I know is he didn't come to work after Wednesday."

"So how was his body discovered?"

"Someone saw on the floor a river of thick, dried blood coming from Kastor's room. Did I mention the door was locked from the inside? It took a dozen men to break it down—"

"A whole dozen?"

"Well, I'm not sure about the exact number, but that's when they heard the droning. A window must have been left open because the floor and walls were covered with bluebottle fl—"

"How was the body identifi—"

"Miriam, why are you peppering me with so many questions?" Looking at me askance, she clutched the beads of her necklace and drew them to her heart. "After all, murder is nothing new in the *Rhakotis* quarter. I mentioned it only because he was your father's clerk for so many years."

"Look, I have a reason," I said with flint in my voice. "How was the body identified? Do you know or not?"

"Okay. Okay." Phoebe waved her hand to brush away our sharp words. "The authorities recognized him as the clerk they knew from the Public Records Office, and don't forget, his overseer had reported him missing on Thursday. But, come to think of it, there was something odd. The *cauponaria* at The Pegasus said Kastor had been calling himself by another name, Kyros or Kleon, something like that."

"Strange." *Or maybe not so strange.* "When was he in the shop last?"

"Hmmm." Phoebe scratched the crown of her head. "He came in to buy some writing supplies on Monday. I remember because I waited on him. He bought a few *calami*—and, by the way, not those ordinary pens but the ones fitted with our most expensive reeds—a bottle of ink, some sealing wax, and a stack of high-quality papyrus sheets. That's all. Nothing more, not like the purchases he'd been making for the Public Records Office.

"Thoth told me all about it, you know—" Phoebe gave me one of her cloak-and-dagger looks. "—how the back of Kastor's head was bashed in, how his face was twisted into a grisly expression of fear and horror. 'Struck down with savage ferocity.' That's what Thoth said. His brains must have drizzled all over the place."

"Phoebe!"

She had a talent for the theatrical. "Okay, okay, but for a spindly guy, Kastor must have put up a really good fight because his body was covered with bruises and scratches."

We lapsed into a thoughtful silence while I wondered why Kastor was killed, but I soon felt Phoebe's eyes boring into me like an awl.

She drained her wine glass but continued to hold me in her stare.

"Miriam…" The pitch and volume of her voice rose

as she stretched out my name. "You're getting that look in your eye, and I don't like it one bit."

I wanted to say "What look?" but my mouth was too dry to speak. Not that it mattered. She could always read my mind.

"I know you! Your mind is spinning like you're about to start another one of your investigations." She threw up her hands and then leaned across the table to lift my chin with her index finger. "Come on, Miriam. Didn't you learn anything from our trip to Caesarea? Like the danger of meddling in other people's business and the value of your own life? Let this go. What happened to Kastor is not your concern. Period."

But I knew it was.

So much so that I completely forgot to tell her about Judah.

# Chapter 12

*Sunday Morning, October 3rd*:

I don't believe in coincidences. Never have. So, after tossing half the night, inventing a hundred explanations, one more implausible than the other, I lumbered out of bed knowing I had to get over to The Pegasus. But rather than have Orestes and Solon take me, I sent them to hire bearers who'd be familiar with the twisting lanes and weed-choked alleys of the *Rhakotis* quarter.

In the meantime, needing her cool hands and serene ways, I called for Calisto to help me dress. I shrugged into a simple, pale yellow, woolen tunic that trailed wooden buttons across the shoulders and down the sleeves and spilled generously over my ankles. Calisto fastened a leather belt about my hips to hike up the hem so the tufts of dung, puddles of excrement, and medallions of phlegm that blotch their rutted streets and byways wouldn't stain the skirt. Next, I worked my feet into my *calcei* and pirouetted so she could make sure the fabric draped evenly before she coiled my hair into a knot, which she anchored to the crown of my head with long copper pins and covered with a net. Finally, she brought me a tray of earrings, bracelets, and rings.

That was when I missed my Phoebe's unflagging intrusiveness. At such times, I could count on her unsolicited, unvarnished, but irksome criticism, especially of my taste. Right off, she'd have forbidden me to wear any jewelry whatsoever. She'd have stirred the air with her index finger while chiding me with, "Who do you think you are? Cleopatra? Remember, Miriam, not everyone plays by your rules. The beggars who line those streets prey on anything that glitters."

And that was when I could also count on her readiness to assist me in one of my investigations by offering her spontaneous, albeit sensational opinions and volunteering her eyes and ears for the places I could not go.

And so, listening to the voice of the Phoebe inside me, I declined the jewelry, asking Calisto to fetch only my himation, the coarse unbleached one at that, which I fastened at my shoulder with a twisted hairpin.

But Orestes and Solon weren't going to return so quickly. Traffic was busiest in the morning, before the still-potent, October sun drenched the streets, and the pavement radiated its heat. Before the shimmer off the stone buildings, statues, and colonnades forced my eyes to the ground. Before the plumes of thirsty air seared my nose and throat. And before the molten light chased the idlers and hawkers, pickpockets and swindlers, street philosophers and soothsayers into the shrinking polygons of precious shade.

Until then, every bearer would be carrying a sedan chair or curtained litter, dodging the soldiers, caravans of camels, and rivers of woolen-cloaked shoppers, their satchels crammed with perfume from Arabia, pottery from Greece, spices from Nubia, and textiles from India. Tourists in their colorful garb would be clogging the Way; bustling about its stalls, tents, and awning-sheltered barrows; and shouting in their native language to be heard over the racket of tinkers, the clang of smiths, the squawk of gulls, and the ever-present throb of soldiers' hobnail boots.

And so I spent the best part of the morning with my fern's crushed leaflets, filtering their tangled veins out of the waters with the expectation that after the waters dried, I could recover their essence for the elixir. Nevertheless, each moment strained my patience.

It was nearly noon by the time Orestes and Solon returned with a polished oak, finial-topped chair, its style verging on ostentation, its back carved in the shapes of seabirds, its arms inlaid with blue jasper and ivory, its wooden seat fitted with a red silk cushion. Carrying it were two of the most unlikely-looking bearers: a bronze-colored, bandy-legged Egyptian with immense hips and a jug-eared youth, his mustache still tentative, his skin abloom with acne, and his left leg withered. Having similar overlapping buck teeth, they looked like father and son.

With no choice, I hired them despite my better judgment. Not only were their bodies ill-suited to their work, but I figured the chair was probably stolen.

I should have listened to my intuition.

Instead, I said nothing beyond negotiating the price for taking me to and from The Pegasus. And I did nothing beyond counting out a few bronze coins from the draw-string purse I kept inside my belt and pressing them into the leader's cupped palm as it rested precariously on the slope that was his belly. Then he held the cushion in place while his young partner seated me.

"Where's the parasol?" I asked, squinting into the fierce sun.

Eliciting only a grunt from one and a twitch from the other, I called to Minta to fetch mine. The parasol, however, turned out to be useless. Once aloft, I needed both hands to grip the right arm of the chair so I could keep myself erect as we listed through the city.

Unable to shade my eyes as the streets unfolded

through the Jewish and *Bruchium* quarters, I missed the pleasurable symmetry of the townhouses and mansions tucked behind long emerald lawns, their arched windows, broad stone steps, and double front doors guarded by fanciful topiary. Only when a team of *pedisequi* stopped us at the Street of the Soma, did I have a chance to unfasten the hairpin at my shoulder, tent the tail of the himation over my head, fashion a brim to shield my eyes, and secure it with the hairpin.

By then, we were in the western outskirts of the *Bruchium* quarter. The villas and estates had given way first to rows of dingy, narrow-chested, faux marble houses with faded roofs and melancholy windows and then to five- and six-story tenements clustered around public fountains encrusted with bird droppings. But I didn't need my eyes to know where we were. I'd heard the rats scuttling, the pigeons squabbling, the stray dogs barking, and the feral cats whining. I'd gagged on the smells of rancid urine, fresh scats, and fried grease. And I'd choked on the geysers of sun-bleached dust.

But we had yet to enter the nameless claustrophobic lanes of the *Rhakotis* quarter. There the toothless idlers would be squatting in gutters littered with rubble. In the shifting shade of tattered garments swinging from a web of clotheslines, they'd be throwing knucklebones and drinking *posca*, a cheap, watered-down, sour wine. And there, the malignant stench of the canal would thicken the air, invade my nostrils, and cling to my clothes.

The stench sharpening as we lurched westward toward the *Kibotos*, the bearers negotiated the gloomy back alleys lined with flat-faced, weather-beaten houses fronted with deeply stained mud bricks and bowed doors propped open with debris. Noah used to call these dwellings boxes of misery. Forlorn even at high noon, pigeons roosting in their lightless windows, they wouldn't let even a blade of light cut between them.

If I'd had a free hand, I could have used the parasol to defend myself when I felt the first pebbles hitting my legs and spotted a gang of guttersnipes taking aim behind the wall of a crumbling tenement. A tangle of skinny brown arms and grimy, eye-filled faces were showering the chair with pebbles, hooting with delight at each hit.

"Can't you go faster?" I yelled as I dared to lean forward so the leader could hear me over the impish whoops of laughter.

Another grunt and twitch but the bearers' pace did quicken. At that point, the urchins darted into the street to chase us half-heartedly. Their feet bare and their knees skinned, they soon came upon a bird-shouldered ragamuffin sweeping out a ditch, a Sisyphean task if there ever was one, and redirected their mischief toward him.

Once we crossed the canal at the *Kibotos*, I heard the toll of buoys, the slap of rigging, and the groan of hawsers. There I found myself in a vaguely familiar maze of still meaner alleys. Instead of ramshackle houses, I saw warehouses, abandoned factories, storage bins—for oil and grain, lumberyards, and slaughterhouses pressed together, the very ones I noticed years ago when I'd gone to The Pegasus looking for a courier headed for Caesarea to take my letter to Judah.

We jerked past a greasy-windowed saloon squatting in an overgrown lot, one of the many that when darkness takes hold, lures a steady stream of sailors, deckhands, and old whores. It's there in those notorious backrooms thrumming with violence that brawls erupt only to end in the canal with a body floating in its own oily streaks of blood. And so I remembered when our gangly tinker, Plato, was stabbed to death while gambling in a nest of lice like that and how his impoverished widow and children had to be sold to slavers to pay his taxes.

And I remembered my shame the night I followed Papa to another such den of depravity. In the meager light of its open door, crouched behind a garbage heap, I watched his self-confidence collapse into desperation. Those were the days when he'd sunk to gambling around a table of ruffians to restore our solvency, at least that's what he told me. But I knew it was to recover his pride, that he'd lost face with Amram and wanted the money to buy out of their partnership. Likewise, I knew in a matter of hours Binyamin and Tychon would be courting their luck in a dive like this. How else could my brother expect to amass the money he needed to buy the *ludus*?

The jolt—and the expletives that followed—when my junior bearer stumbled into a pothole roused me from my grim recollections. I chased away my images of dark, pungent saloons, gambling dens, and ruffians as the chair swayed to a halt in front of a sign depicting the winged, white stallion's birth.

The horizon lurched as I climbed out of the lowered chair, but I clung to its arms until I could blink the ground to a standstill. Once steadied, I wiped my damp palms on the skirt of my tunic to count out an extra bronze coin to persuade the bearers to wait for me.

"Perhaps an hour," I said. "Maybe a little longer."

Another grunt and twitch from the bearers and I turned to make my way along the sinuous, dust-fouled walkway lined with blighted shrubs. The overhead branches of the towering plane trees creaked mournfully as I passed through the rusty gate, skirted the bar—where the voices were masculine and the talk was vulgar—and came upon the mural of Bellerophon's flight on Pegasus, smaller than I remembered, and the scarred oak door that cut through the stallion's wing.

As soon as the door screeched open but before I could smell the rancid oil in the ring of lamps suspended from the public room's planked ceiling, I noticed my mother's fibula pinned to the waist of the potbellied dwarf I recognized as Nathaniel ben Ruben.

# CHAPTER 13

*Sunday Afternoon, October 3rd*:

As if time had hurtled me backward, I saw Nathaniel ben Ruben as I had eight years ago, dozing on a wooden stool, his squat body propped up in a corner against a slanting wall, his chin tucked, his feet dangling above an earthenware chamber pot. Only the graying Hebraic beard that once splayed across his barrel chest had thinned to a yellowish-white fluff, and the deeply-etched lines under his closed eyes had thickened to pouches.

Likewise, the public room was essentially unchanged. The air was heavy with the same odors of sour linen, stale henket, and that indescribable stench of kitchen garbage. *Unless that's the tang of their upcoming dinner*, I thought sardonically. And the room itself had succumbed to only a more profound gloom: its walls duller, darker, and pressing closer; its corners thicker with soot and grime; and its uncertain light ever more menacing. But I wasn't so appalled this time recalling that my brother had stayed in this greasy box. On the contrary, the splotches of peeling paint and the fading frescoes veiled with cobwebs seemed suited the Binyamin who'd just come home.

But then, shaking my head, I reminded myself: *I'm not here to brood about Binyamin. I'm here to find out whether Kastor had anything to do with the disappearance of Amram's will.* I suspected he had and hoped to find the evidence, or better yet, the will itself. After all, why would Kastor, a public slave, desert his post, an offense punishable by the *summum supplicium*, the most extreme punishment? If the Romans chose crucifixion, his body would hang under a scorching sun until it was consumed by birds of prey. If they chose *damnatio ad bestias*, he'd be thrown to the wild beasts. In either case, he'd suffer the greatest dishonor of all: With no body to bury, he'd be denied a funeral, and his soul would never find peace.

The dwarf must have sensed either my gaze or my shifting shadow across the pitted earthen floor because his snores cut off abruptly and his eyes snapped open. Where his dream had taken him I do not know, but only after studying the grime in one of the corners, did he seem to remember he was in the public room of The Pegasus. And then, with the precision of a choreographed dance, he jumped off the stool, scratched his potbelly, retched into the chamber pot, and wiped his mouth on his sleeve.

A shower of crumbs dropped from his beard.

When he craned his neck, I couldn't tell whether his bronze weathered face was directed at me or the Almighty until he said, "Blessed be His name."

His sonorous voice so belied his stature and our shabby surroundings that I had to smile.

"It's Zemirah," he exclaimed, and as if the Almighty needed an explanation, he added, "the beautiful maiden who paid me so generously for carrying her letter to Caesarea!"

"Miriam," I said, correcting him. "Miriam bat Isaac."

"Yes, of course. Miriam. I most humbly beg your pardon." He bowing deeply only to spot a rat as big as a dog scuttle toward the kitchen. Shaking his stick to no avail except to vent his frustration, he closed his eyes with an extravagant sigh.

He spoke again once his breathing slowed to normal. "With your charity, I bought this handsomest of walking sticks, one that proudly bears the marks of having saved my lowly life more than once."

Squaring his shoulders, holding onto the brass knob with his meaty hand, he extended the stick for my approval. The brass was made from the usual proportion of calamine and copper. The stick itself was oak, about two feet long, stout, weighted, probably with lead, and shod with iron.

"Yes, a handsome companion indeed," I said, tracing my index finger along its cracks, one still raw but the others cured to a shiny black. "And I see it's served you well."

"You know, I'm an itinerant. I carry valuables from city to city. But travel in Judea has become even more perilous than when I last saw you." His face pinched into a forlorn expression. "Peasant gangs roving the highways," he explained as if I might not otherwise understand.

"The Romans call them bandits and thugs, but they're really just pitiable beggars, the unemployed shepherds and displaced farmers, thieves by desperation armed with their own cudgels, hunting bows, and slingshots." He shoulders rounded with pity as he spoke. "Still, they lurk in ravines and caves to prey on the likes of me. So I've had to use this stick to defend myself."

*And quite recently*, I thought.

"You wouldn't recognize Judea now, Zemirah—"

"Miriam."

"Yes. Miriam." He bowed again, this time not so deeply. "The small subsistence farms are gone. Swallowed up. Consolidated into a few huge estates. And our new Roman-fed aristocracy? You should see how their purses bulge with newly-minted Roman coins.

"How did this happen?" But I knew.

He ignored my question. His own thoughts had overtaken him and poured out in a torrent.

"In the meantime, the frustrations of the dispossessed have mushroomed, especially since Passover when the *Sicarii* assassinated the High Priest under the very noses of six hundred Roman soldiers. Tell me, what were these formidable warriors doing? Polishing their cuirasses in the Antonia Fortress?" His sarcasm rang with bitterness. "One swipe across Jonathan's throat was all it took."

Ben Ruben mimed a swipe with his index finger.

"Buoyed by their success, their ranks swelling, the *Sicarii* see themselves now more than ever as heroes, as Almighty's revolutionary force committed to ridding the land of its impious invaders."

His pulse throbbed at his temples.

"So they rob and murder at will. And not just the Romans, mind you, but the Jews thought to be collaborating with them and anyone else like me carrying valuables."

He leaned against the stool and rested his left elbow on the seat, which told me his lecture was over.

Except for the buzz of a frantic fly spiraling about the room, the silence expanded as I debated with myself whether to bring up the fibula. And then, before I knew it, my lips spouted these words:

"I see you have a handsome fibula as well."

"Yes, I have that too." His right hand dropped either to caress his precious clasp or shield it from my gaze. I couldn't tell which.

He said nothing more. So I postponed my questions until I could check with Binyamin, who as much as told me he had our mother's fibula and would give it back to me after his bout on Wednesday. After all, I told myself, *many fibulas could look like our mother's, especially in these flickering shadows*.

"Now, young lady, as much as I'd like to help you, I hope you're not going to ask me to carry another letter to Caesarea." He waggled his head with a drawn face and brooding eyes. "After decades of accusations and insults over who rightfully owns the city, the Jews and Greeks have taken to the streets to settle the matter. I tell you, there's a bone-deep gash in that city. It's gushing blood, and the discharge is putrid."

"I'm so sorry. I had the chance to visit, you know, such a splendid city, the harbor, the statues flanking its entrance, and the Drusion—" *Though the Pharos Lighthouse is three times taller.* "—all built within twelve years. Can you believe that? Only twelve years! And the *Cardo Maximus*, so much like our Canopic Way—" I couldn't stop babbling. "—the elegant shops, the charming teahouses, the—"

My fast-flowing words sounded as false as the lines of a bad actor.

So I pulled in a long breath and started again.

"I'm here because my uncle's former slave died here a couple of days ago. His name was Kastor, but he also went by another name, Kyros or Kleon, something like that. If you saw him, you'd know him; he had a clubfoot. My uncle was very fond of Kastor and asked me to find out how he died so he could make a gift to anyone who helped Kastor during his last days." My lie tasted hot as it slid off my tongue. "Did you by any chance know him?"

"I actually did, the new tenant you mean. In fact, his room was next to mine. I tried to make friends with him. Really I did. You know my business depends on making contacts, but he kept to himself, made it clear he wanted to be left alone. He was here for just a few days, well maybe two, three at the most. So, I can't say I helped him unless you'd count leaving him alone."

"Well, I wonder if I could see his room."

"That's the *cauponaria*'s business, Fabia, our tarty, somewhat worn hostess. We call her our very own Venus." A playful smile curved his lips before crinkling his entire face.

But then, after combing his fingers through his beard, he looked up at me with mischievous eyes and lowered his voice to a collusive whisper. "Most afternoons immediately after lunch, the *cauponaria* announces she's going to the agora, but I know better. You can hear her entertaining one ship captain or another in her room behind the kitchen. If you dare go into the kitchen, that is." His mouth widened into a toothy grin as his eyes swept toward the back of the inn. "Well, my room is just above hers, so I know what goes on. Her voice takes on a husky lilt, as if her words could melt a stone, and whoever her caller happens to be, you can count on his words shredding the air with vulgarisms."

The corners of his parted lips turned down. "Fabia left for the agora a while ago." He rolled his eyes when he said *agora*. "So we don't have much time, but I could take you upstairs, and if someone sees us, we could just pretend you've taken a special liking to me."

He shot me a conspiratorial wink, I consented with a tight-lipped nod, and that was how I found myself sneaking up the stairs of a seamy, rat-infested inn with a man half my size and twice my age.

ꟹ

We sealed our pact with an exchange of giggles and *shushes* whereupon my new-found friend tiptoed over to a long, wooden trestle table and bench among the many strewn about the room. Following him with my eyes aided by an apron of light from one of the ceiling lamps, I watched him climb onto the bench, stand, and belly across the table to filch two candles from the candelabrum.

Tiptoeing back, the candles held high, he dragged the stool under the ring of lamps and mimed for me to climb up and light one of the candles from the single lingering flame. I unwrapped my himation, letting it puddle onto the floor, and hiked up the skirt of my tunic another inch while ben Ruben positioned himself to steady the stool. Next, lifting my knees onto the seat, pulling myself up, and then standing with hardly a teeter, I fixed my gaze to keep my balance and reached for the lamp's uncertain flame until the candle flared to life. As I stepped down, my friend took the candle from my lowered hand, used it to light the other one, and with a few jerks of his head toward the stairwell, signaled we'd better hurry.

He led the way through a scrim of cobwebs to a steep spiral of narrow, warped steps. A few dim lanterns furry with dust released a strong resinous odor as they lay a yellowish skin on the walls of the stairwell. The shadows leaped and shuddered like ghosts with the trembling of my hand while the echo of our footsteps followed me up the stairs to a corridor reeking of urine and desperation.

When I paused on the landing, heartened by the bars of lesser darkness beneath some of the rude plank doors, ben Ruben whispered over his shoulder, "Are you all right?"

I managed a crisp nod while pressing my index finger to my lips, but his whisper and the creak of the floorboards had already alerted his neighbors. They opened their doors a crack, and like turtles with their necks protruding, they poked their hideous faces around the doorjamb. A moment later, after a slow blink or soft sigh, their faces relaxed, and they retreated into their shells. No doubt they'd been alarmed by Kastor's murder. As each door closed, I missed the wedge of light but not the room's foul breath.

I trailed behind ben Ruben's substantial shoulders imagining I was dragging myself up the *Diolkos*, the ramp the Greeks built to haul their ships across the Isthmus of Corinth. But even with that flight of fancy and the meager light from some of the doorsills, I could still tell which room had been Kastor's by tracing the dark brown river painted on the floorboards. Still, the slope of the floor was insufficient to account for the length of the stain. Clearly the blood must have gushed, which told me Phoebe had hardly exaggerated. The attack had indeed been ferocious. Kastor must have bled to death from a ruptured artery before or after his skull was fractured. In other words, his death was far from instantaneous.

I had to swallow twice when ben Ruben found Kastor's door locked. Had I really expected us to troop right into a crime scene? Kastor was a public slave; his murder, the destruction of state property. The Romans would see to it that someone paid for their loss. But just as I was about to write off the trip as useless, ben Ruben, standing on tiptoe and with his weight behind one shoulder, forced the door open a crack. Then, using his opposite hand to insert his stick into the breach, he levered up the wooden bar.

I must say I was surprised, even startled by the strength of this little man, so much so that I could hear

Phoebe scolding me. "For the love of Isis, Miriam, this time you've gone too far! Upstairs in a sleazy inn with a man strong enough to drag you into his *cella*, kill you with one stroke of his stick, which I might add you bankrolled, and in the dead of night, dump your body into the canal." I could picture her shaking her index finger at me until, her voice croaking and her arms akimbo, she summed up her frustration: "How many narrow escapes does it take for you to learn not to venture into the *Rhakotis* quarter alone?"

*But, Phoebe, I didn't come alone. My bearers are waiting for—Well, I* hope *my bearers are waiting for me.*

I shivered when the open door exhaled the coppery odor of dried blood.

ꕥꕥ

The room was shrouded in darkness save for the thin strips of sunlight that knifed through the slats of the shuttered window. I heard a thump, the clunk of a stick, and another of ben Ruben's extravagant sighs while, with candle in hand, I groped my way to the window. When I folded back the shutters, the light scissored through a tangle of silvery leaves to reveal a narrow, somber *cella* and an eddy of dust motes.

Ben Ruben had taken a seat on the edge of the naked cot, its mattress spattered with dried blood, a flanged chamber pot on the floor beneath the bed frame. The flame from his candle, which he'd planted in a stone holder next to the cot, sent up spirals of black smoke and dusted his cheek with an orange sheen. Kicking the air with each swing of his stubby legs, he held his stick between parted knees, his hands layered around its knob, its tip poking the floor. A wicker trunk and bench across from the cot completed the room's sad furnishings.

First, I wanted to examine the floor. Hunkering down, I began by observing the blood stain near the door. If Kastor had been struck from behind, a reasonable assumption based on Phoebe's account, he'd probably been trying to get away. Then, on the door itself, I saw across its width a line of bloody blobs, each with a tail cascading to the floor. As I circled the room, I saw various patterns, some drips small and round, others larger, even irregular like tear drops, with their own constellation of spatters on not only the floor but the furniture, even the window sill.

Curious but then I remembered the room had been locked from the inside.

Suddenly, a thunderous shriek split the air, sending its vibrations up through the floor to rattle the chamber pot. Whether the last gasp of a dying man or one in the throes of ecstasy, I could not tell until I glanced at ben Ruben.

"Quick! That means they're finished. In a minute, Fabia will spot your himation and come upstairs to surprise the prostitute who must have left it and exact a heavy tax for the use of her facilities." He rolled his eyes again when he said her facilities.

"Wait! I must see what's inside the trunk." *Could Amram's will be there? Or any other clue as to why Kastor was killed?* "But you, Mr. ben Ruben, you must leave now. You've already put yourself in enough danger. Hurry."

"But Zemirah—"

"No! Go now!"

As I pushed him out the door, I heard a pounding on the stairs and spied an oversized head curtained with lanky, orangey hair rising in the stairwell. A heavy set of chins slung like necklaces over a pair of boxy shoulders materialized next, followed in turn by pendulous breasts, wide hips, and thick ankles.

As soon as she reached the landing, she lumbered down the hall toward me.

I froze long enough to notice nesting in her cleavage on a long, silk cord an L-shaped latch lifter with an iron shaft and a couple of teeth on the end.

The wide sleeve of her robe caught on a splintery doorjamb.

I hoped that would slow her down.

But it didn't.

Her sleeve ripped instead,

And she kept on going.

As soon as she entered the first room, I eased Kastor's door closed until I heard the latch click.

A drop of sweat trailed down my back and turned to ice. I pivoted on my heels and rushed to the trunk. I lifted the lid and plunged the candle into the darkness to see what was there. No sense sticking my hand in without checking, right? I'd learned that lesson in Caesarea.

I'd hoped to find Amram's will, but instead I found only a smooth board that could have been used as a writing surface, and the pens, sealing wax, papyrus, and bottle of ink Phoebe mentioned. Trifles but they must have been important for Kastor to have brought them here.

I could understand why he might have come here, but why had he stayed here? And why had he left his position at the Public Records Office? So, I wanted to look for anything else he might have brought.

But I could feel Fabia's footfalls shifting the floorboards and hear their groan. She was already at the door, working the latch. Stunned by the moment, I didn't know what to do.

My heart kept punching inside my chest. I looked around conscious of only my own confusion. And then I dropped the trunk lid, pitched the candle into the chamber pot, and ran to the window.

I had no choice.

She'd lifted the latch.

And so, just as Binyamin had taught me, I backed against the window, gripped the sill, and hoisted myself up until I could perch there. Then turning to face the trees, I leaned out, paddled through the leaves, grabbed the firmest limb I could reach, and swung out. Hanging there, moving hand to hand from bough to bough, I dropped down until I could swoop to the ground.

I landed in a clump of sickly, sour-smelling weeds pocked with pigeon excrement.

*No use looking for footprints from last Friday.*

Besides, the *cauponaria* was calling out to me. But the foliage was too thick for her to get more than a peek.

And she wasn't about to follow.

I looked for the bearers, but they, along with my parasol, were gone. And of course, I'd left my himation behind. All I had were the shingles of bark and scraps of blood-streaked leaves that clung to me like patches.

But I could still rely on the lighthouse, its limestone façade painted orange by the late-afternoon sun. It had guided me through this frightful neighborhood before. I had only my imagination to fear: the canopy of darkness that turned out to be only a cloud of passing sand martins, the bloodthirsty tabby that sought only a scratch between its ears, and the purple-tongued mastiff that, hackles up, tracked me but only to the shade of a nearby alley.

When I finally crossed the canal and entered the *Bruchium* quarter, I hailed a sedan chair and thought the whole way home about how to approach Binyamin about the fibula.

# CHAPTER 14

*Monday, late morning, October 4th*:

The air in Binyamin's suite, ripe with the odors of sweat and tension, brought me back to our childhood when I'd visit him in the evenings, sometimes to share our accomplishments, mine academic, his athletic, but more often to vent our frustrations and tally our grievances against Papa. I'd be afraid Binyamin would ask me to back up another one of his lies, but on that late morning in October, I was afraid he'd tell me something I didn't want to hear about our mother's fibula.

When he waved me in, I saw the room as he'd left it a decade ago. Only his boyhood athletic equipment, his barbells, bench, exercise mat, and discus, had been moved into his *cubiculum* to make room for the crate he'd brought from Capua. Fans of light from the windows illuminated the eddies of disorder and spun an amber glow on his austere furnishings: a sleeping couch, chamber pot, freestanding brass candlestick, wicker chair, and cedar wardrobe, its doors open, his tunics, sandals, and boots spilling onto the mosaic floor.

In the early stages of getting dressed—or undressed—he was loosely wrapped in a short-sleeved, silk robe open to the waist. Slouched in his chair, his breakfast tray on the couch still untouched—the cream had already formed a skin on his porridge—he was working instead on an amphora of some foul-smelling, fermented beverage.

His body and jowls looked more bloated than usual, his skin more papery, his eyes more restless, but aside from that and the stubble that smudged his cheeks, chin, and neck, he seemed no better or worse than when he first arrived.

He had the same indelible tattoos, the same long-standing scars, and the same impudent manner.

"To what do I owe this most noble visit?" he said, slurring his words as he sat back in his chair and clasped his hands behind his head.

I ignored his sarcasm.

"I just wanted to take a peek at our mother's fibula. Of course, you'll keep it for your bout, but the truth is

I've been longing to get it back. And now that it's almost time, I'm eager to see it."

"Listen, Sis," he said leaning forward, spreading his hands in a gesture of helplessness, "I'm kind of busy right n—"

"No problem." I shrugged. "Just tell me where it is. I'll get it later." I heard myself speaking faster and in a higher pitch than I'd rehearsed. I warned myself to slow down, but my tongue wasn't heeding my advice. "And I'll put it right back. Honest. I promise."

"I'll have to look for it. Right now, I can't find anything in this mess." He extended his arm and swept the air with a sigh. "I haven't had time even to unpack since I came home. Everything is still in a jumble—Which reminds me, the maids don't do anything around here. You're too soft on them. You've spoiled them. I'd have sold them to the *ludus* years ago, Phoebe included, not that any of them would have lasted in the arena." A snicker joggled his boyhood scar.

Surely, he was joking. No one could be that pitiless.

He slumped back in his chair, drained the amphora with a shiver, and tossed it into the chamber pot.

Dropping down onto the edge of the couch, I pushed aside his soiled linen so I could inch forward and fix my eyes on his.

"Look, Sis, don't divert me—"

"Binny, I wasn't try—"

"But you are. So just tell me. Why do you really

want to see the fibula? Don't you believe I have it?"

"All right," I blurted out. "I thought I saw someone wearing it yesterday, someone at The Pegas—"

He threw up his hands. "The Pegasus? So, you thought you saw someone wearing it at The Pegasus!" he mimicked. "You've got to be kidding! Listen, you're mistaken. Even you, my brilliant sister, might not know everything. That fibula may have looked like our mother's, but I assure you—" His body stiffened as his palm flew to his chest. "—I have hers safely tucked away somewhere in this clutter."

His eyes slid away.

Was it then that my distrust blossomed, or was it when he so swiftly changed the subject?

"Anyway, what on Earth were you doing there?"

"Well, I know you're in a hurry, and it's a long story—"

"No, I'm interested. Tell me."

A fierce disgust churned in my innards, but I resolved to stay in the vain hope I could find out how the fibula ended up at The Pegasus. So I asked him: "Do you remember Papa's secretary, Kastor?"

Binyamin contracted his brows to affect a puzzled look.

"The one with the clubfoot," I prompted.

"Vaguely." He folded his arms across his chest. "So, what if I do?"

"Well, he was killed there last Friday. Savagely

murdered, clubbed to death in his room, the stink of his blood everywhere." I tried to impersonate Phoebe, but lacking her flair for histrionics, my voice sounded flat and unfamiliar, as if I'd memorized the words.

"Well, that just shows you. You can't trust anybody in the *Rhakotis* quarter. But why is that your business? Kastor hasn't worked for us in years."

"I know, but Amram's will mysteriously disappeared from his box in the Public Records Office, and Kastor was in charge of those boxes. So, I was thinking there could be a connection between the two."

"Between what two?"

"Between Kastor's murder and the disappearance of the will. As Amram's partner and financial manager, it's my responsibility to see that he has a will."

See, I too could be imperious.

"So, why don't you just draw up another?"

"Well, until I know how and why it disappeared, the same thing could happen again. Besides, I'm curious. I can't imagine why anybody would steal it."

He rubbed the stubble on his chin with his fingertips. "Well, who's the beneficiary?"

"I am."

"The *sole* beneficiary?" He arched his eyebrows in mock surprise while pinching his mouth into a smirk. "So that's why you're so concerned!"

"Being the sole beneficiary simply means Amram trusts me to continue distributing his assets in accord with his wishes." My chin lifted as I spoke. "And as for Kastor, he may have been a bitter complainer—and I certainly didn't like him—but his death should still be avenged." Before the silence between us could harden, I stood to leave mumbling something like, "Well, I know you're busy."

But later I'd ask myself: *Was there any way I could have foreseen that my mention of the fibula and Kastor would pitch my brother over the edge?*

# Chapter 15

*Tuesday, October 5th*:

So much happened once I got to The Pegasus that I could remember very little about that morning. I'd asked Orestes and Solon to take me in the chair because whether or not I might need their protection, I could count on their waiting, no matter how long it might take for me to recover the fibula and find out how it came to be pinned to the waist of my new undersized friend.

I was so rarely late, though, that I remember Orestes calling to me. "Miss Miriam, the sun's already scaling the courtyard fence."

Solon might have still been polishing the mahogany poles on the sedan chair—his time passed more slowly than anyone else's—but I could picture Orestes, sparkling with energy, pacing back and forth under the portico. At that moment, I was in the atrium, leaning over the edge of the bench, checking my reflection in the pool.

I'd done everything I could to look different from the limber prostitute Fabia imagined seeing through the blur of leaves on Sunday. Not that she'd recognize me, but someone at the bar might. Minta dressed me in a silky, light blue himation over my brighter blue linen tunic, plaited my hair with ribbons into one thick braid to trail over my shoulder, a hairdo I rarely wore. Then she painted my lips and cheeks with red ochre and blackened my eyebrows with ashes. But I had to chuckle when she held the bronze mirror up to my face. With the cosmetics, I looked more than ever like a prostitute. So Minta had to unwrap my himation, open the clasps across the shoulders of my tunic, lower the bodice, wash my face, and then put me back together again. So that's why Orestes had to wait until the sun was grazing the top of the fence before I was ready to leave.

I remembered once we reached the Canopic Way, my ears grabbed the words of the public criers announcing the games, and my gaze captured the posters carried by the organizers' special slaves. The realization that gladiatorial combat would begin tomorrow cut through me like the keen edge of a dagger. The larger ads, those in both Latin and Greek painted in red on the walls of the buildings, specified the *familia gladiatoria*, the number of bouts, and each day's gifts, the foods and coins, vases and jugs, animal skins and olive oil that could be redeemed with the lottery tokens thrown into the arena after the show.

Next the ads listed each day's events featuring exotic animals from every corner of the Empire. Tomorrow, monkeys would ride dogs, sea lions would bark on cue, and the *noxii* sentenced to death by *damnatio ad bestias* would be tied to a stake and torn apart by bears or bulls, lions or tigers. But the most popular animal event was when unmounted hunters demonstrated their skill against the wildest beasts with a javelin, spear, or bow and arrow.

While Orestes and Solon jostled their way through the usual horde of soothsayers, street philosophers, and beggars, I looked for Binyamin's name on an ad posted above the carved oak door of a vine-laced, private townhouse that during the games offers kitchen privileges along with lodging to upcountry travelers. Only when I recalled that Binyamin's nom de guerre was Agrippa Fortitudo, could I find him listed on the first day's lineup, and then I spotted Tychon's on the second. That's when I realized that tonight, he and Tychon would be attending the *cena libera*, the banquet on the eve of the games for all participating gladiators. So even if I recovered the fibula, I wouldn't be able to give it to him before his bout.

As we made our way past the fountains and monuments, sphinxes and statues that grace the Way, I tried to concentrate on the splendor of the buildings: the double-colonnaded basilica of the Great Synagogue, the grove of marble columns that fronts the Great Gymnasium, and the marble dome of the Museum's circular dining hall. But my mind kept veering off into the orbit that was the fibula, the one item that had been in our family for generations, the one item my mother meant for me to have. The thought that ben Ruben might no longer have it unnerved me so much that I couldn't focus on how I was going to recover it, never mind how ben Ruben got it or how he was connected to my brother. But I knew I was going to have to get to the bottom of those posers too.

Soon we approached the narrow, menacing lanes of the *Rhakotis* quarter, Orestes's boots setting the pace while Solon's scuffed up plumes of dust. Despite the warmth of the morning's honeyed light, the gloom of the crumbling mud-brick buildings stippled my skin. I noticed our pace quickening once we crossed the canal, even Solon's boots beating a steady rhythm as he and Orestes loped along the waterfront accompanied by the mournful moan of the sea. And then, as soon as I called "Here!" they lowered the chair at the foot of the walkway to the inn.

Upon passing through the gate and reaching the door, I realized that like Bellerophon, I too was on my way to kill the Chimera, only I didn't have the spear or block of lead to slay the monster.

ᏒᏒ

I didn't see his face at first, just the coils of smoke from the lanterns in the stairway writhing in the wake of his enormous flat feet clopping down the steps. And then it was too late. I'd tucked myself into the alcove behind the stairwell, my eyes frantically searching for ben Ruben, hoping he could save me. But no, Tychon was already greeting me like a long-lost cousin.

"Hey, 'member me? With Agrip'." He compressed his syllables and slobbered as if his tongue were too big for his mouth while a dozen pairs of curious eyes bored into me.

I turned to face him. What else could I do, cornered in the dusty shadows like that, his monolithic frame spanning the space, trapping me in my refuge, his fetid breath brushing my face? "Forgive me, Tychon, I didn't recognize you." His face was so swollen, his arms scored with so many scratches that I could have been telling the truth. "It's so nice to see you again." I was making a mammoth effort to sound affable, to mask the detestation that crawled inside me like a worm, but even so, an oily shrillness had crept into my voice.

"Been practicing with a *doctor* in your *ludus*." That didn't make any sense—he was after all from a rival *ludus*—but in his next breath, before I had a chance to question him, he said, "Agrip' didn't tell me you were coming."

"Who?"

"Your brother."

And by then, my question was gone.

"I'm here to visit my friend, Nathaniel ben Ruben. Have you seen him?"

"That dwarf who killed Kleon, Kastor, whatever his name? You heard about their fight, right?"

"About what?"

"The fight. They had a fight."

I leaned toward him, squinting as if I could better understand him that way. Not only was my pulse thudding so loudly that I could hardly hear him, but he was clipping his vowels and swallowing his words before I could make sense of them.

"Not much," I lied. "Let's go outside. You can tell me more."

I elbowed my way through the motley gathering of onlookers to follow Tychon beyond the stink of unwashed bodies, soiled linen, and moldy food to the reek of the waterfront, its putrid seaweed, raw sewage, and brine. He earned a scowl from the hound-faced counterman as he filched a bench from the bar and carried it toward the gate. Planting it in a patch of ripple grass that had invaded the walkway, he beckoned me with a wave of his hand.

A twinge of fear rippled through me when I sat down to face him, the blaze of the late morning sun limning the burly physique of a condemned killer hardly an arm's length away. "So what happened between Kastor and Mr. ben Ruben?" I prompted, as if he'd forgotten why I wanted to speak with him and was imagining instead we were sharing an intimate dinner in The Flamingo's Tongue, about to sample their signature dish.

"Began soon after Kastor settled in. Tuesday or Wednesday."

"Which?"

"Must've been Wednesday, after your brother and I left."

"Are you sure?" I could hear Phoebe warning me not to pepper him with so many questions, to just let him talk.

"Had to be. Two days later he was killed. Yeah, late Wednesday."

An awkward pause threatened to stretch into a grim silence while he chewed on a hangnail and spit it out.

"And?"

As I listened to his ramblings, especially his story about Kastor's last night, I missed many of his words as they got caught in his ever tightening throat. But I didn't dare interrupt his account for clarification. The mindless mashing of his thighs with his huge, freshly scabbed hands as well as the glitter of moisture on his brow further confirmed my judgment that he was highly agitated.

"Everyone heard them: Kastor accusing the dwarf of hounding him, asking him annoying questions and the dwarf saying he was just trying to be friendly, that Kastor was too secretive or sensitive, I forget which."

"So, they bickered." I shrugged. "Is that all?"

"No, only the beginning. Thursday morning, at the bar, they had another, this time vicious argument. The rumor is—I wasn't there, but I have ears—the rumor is Kastor was having breakfast when the dwarf sat down beside him. Everyone says Kastor began to burn with anger, and when he hurled out a few choice words, some threatening, he sprayed the dwarf with his spittle. So the dwarf raised his stick—some say he poked Kastor—and called him names, cripple or gimp, something like that. And that's when Kastor bared his teeth—the counterman said you could see every tooth in his head—and this Kastor or Kleon or whatever his name was bellowed such a string of curses in so many languages that everyone in the public room froze. Must've been the last straw for the dwarf because he smacked his fist on the counter and Kastor's breakfast—porridge, crockery, and all—went flying."

Tychon took a deep breath and looked at me as if to see whether I'd been duly impressed by his story.

So I nodded.

"And then, that night, yes, I'm sure. Thursday night." His voice had dropped to a whisper. "Kastor by then must have been infuriated. I saw him sneak into the dwarf's room late that night and steal his walking stick. To torment him. Why else would anyone take a stick that short?"

"But it was so late. How could you see all that?"

"Our rooms are in a row. First mine by the landing, next the dwarf's, then Kastor's." One by one, he counted off the three rooms on the fingers of one hand.

"That night, your brother and I had been out late. He wanted me to meet Sergius. See if we could squeeze some money out of him. Met him at a cookshop near the canal. This Sergius, the famous one-armed gladiator. I mean he was a gladiator before he lost his arm, and now he's an agent for *lanistae*. Even though he was sorry he didn't have the cash for a stake in our *ludus*, he offered to sell us gladiators and *doctores* whenever we wanted. Real nice, this guy. Bought us all the henket we could drink and all the grilled lamb we could eat. You should have seen how much your brother ate."

He exploded with a guffaw.

By this time, though, I was getting weary, trying to follow his prate.

"When Sergius refused, your brother grimaced as if he'd been gored. And even though he tried to push the pain inside, the frustration was there in his thinned lips and those blue veins throbbing at his temples. So when we left and were about to go our separate ways, I said, just meaning to comfort him, 'At least we can still count on Sergius for some things.' Well, you should have seen him flare up, your brother. I won't repeat what he said, but his words slashed the air like a *sica.* Then he pulled off a *calceus* and hurled it over the cookshop's street-side counter, smashing a shelf of glassware and a clay wine jar to smithereens. I'll bet the mummies in the main necropolis heard that!"

Tychon's story rekindled my memory of that Shabbat evening so long ago when Binyamin hurled his leather sandals at our father's collection of antique Etruscan vases.

"That brother of yours, he's really something," he added, emerging from his story with another guffaw.

"So how did you happen to see Kastor steal ben Ruben's walking stick?"

"Well, I'm getting to that," he snapped. He must have noticed my foot jiggling. "Like I said, I got home late that night. I wasn't sleepy, so I sat by the window watching the moon rise until it was like this silver ball hanging in the treetops. That's when I heard this creak of branches and twigs scratch the siding. So I turned my gaze and noticed that nimble fool Kastor climbing into the dwarf's room. Like I said, they're all in a row, our rooms and the trees too.

"I put my ear to the wall. Nothing except the dwarf snoring. I even peeped through the cracks. Too dark. So I went back to my window. Before long—the moon had hardly budged—I heard that same dreary creaking and scratching and caught a glimpse of Kastor again, this time with something hanging from his belt. I knew it was the dwarf's walking stick because as Kastor slipped back into his room, the moonlight gathered on the brass knob."

"So what do you think it means?"

"That crazy dwarf killed Kastor. Everybody knows that. To get his stick back. Maybe he didn't mean to. Who knows? But he did." With that, he shifted his weight, slapped his thighs, and stood. I noticed he winced as if he'd hurt his back, but without another word, he strode toward the gate.

Cradling my elbow, I rested my chin on the back of my hand for a few minutes and closed my eyes against the sun, aware of the need to think logically but unable to make much sense of what I'd heard. Then flexing my legs to ease their stiffness, I rose to my feet, and stumbling over myself, my mind spinning with possibilities, I toddled back to the inn to look for ben Ruben. With more questions than ever, I wondered why Tychon, a man who hoards every word, had so much to say to me.

ꕥ

As soon as I reached the mural of Bellerophon's flight, I heard footsteps overtaking me, their rapid rhythm punctuated by the grinding of a walking stick against the sand.

"Zemirah, is that you?" he called, panting. "Has the Almighty blessed me once again with your company?"

"Yes, Mr. ben Ruben, but I'm the one blessed," I said as I whirled around.

The first thing I noticed was the fibula pinned to his waist.

*Praise to the Lord, he still has it.* Then I saw he was carrying a satchel of sundries: candles, incense, and natron, but given his stoop and the heft of his bag, he might have had a few amphorae of wine in there too.

"Actually, I'm hoping you have time to chat with me. How about that bench?"

His eyes followed my finger, and he bowed.

I tried to relieve him of his bag. The beads of perspiration across his forehead told me he must have carried it all the way from the agora, considerably more than a mile, but whether out of habit, pride, or some protective instinct, he held fast to the handles.

"So, young lady, I'm most eager to be of service to you," he said, as he placed his bag near the end of the bench. Then hoisting himself up and settling into an island of light, he took the place that had been Tychon's, his knees facing mine, his hands lowered to the knob of his stick, its tip poking into the ripple grass.

"I'm still acting on behalf of my uncle, looking to reward anyone here who might have befriended Kastor. You see, my uncle is aware that Kastor was often surly, even belligerent, especially to strangers. That's why I'm looking for anyone who might have been kind to him. Maybe you saw someone with him."

His shoulders slumped forward, and he heaved a sigh of regret. "Yes, I was with him, but we quarreled, though I certainly didn't intend to. In fact, I wanted to be of service to him not only because that's my business but out of a sense of kinship with him. After all, we both have had to live with a physical limitation that's subjected us to the stings of mockery. And so I thought he'd welcome my friendship. Instead, and to my chagrin, he first accused me of stalking him, even spying on him, though for what purpose I cannot imagine, and then the following morning, he cursed me, even threatened me. Again, I cannot fathom why."

"If my uncle could, he would apologize for Kastor." Leaning in, I maintained the steady look that's indispensable to any good liar. "Did you happen to see him with anyone else?" I figured I may as well continue with my cover story, but dipping his chin, my friend closed his eyes and waggled his head. And then, just as I wondered where to go next, the fibula or the walking stick, he made the choice for me.

"But now I have a question for you, Zemirah," he said, pointing at me with the long, ragged nail of his index finger. "I notice your eyes keep alighting on the fibula I'm wearing. I know you've admired it, but is there any other reason you keep looking at it?"

"Well, there is. I see it belonged to a Roman citizen. So I know there must be an interesting story behind how you got it."

"Now surely you have better ways to spend your afternoon than listening to an old goat reminisce about how he got his trinkets. I have so many, you know, some made by craftsmen in the agora here or the forum in Caesarea. They're all souvenirs, you know, of my travels. As a matter of fact, I saw a matron, short—well not like me but wearing a similar one. Well, not exactly—"

"Please, Mr. ben Ruben, I need to know its provenance. I believe it was my mother's. It's been in my family for three generations but has recently gone missing, and its disappearance has plunged me into the deepest gloom. You see, my mother meant for me to have it with the expectation that I would pass it on to my own daughter." I felt a tingle in my chin when I said that. "So that's why I'd like to know how you got it, to find out how it disappeared. But regardless, I'm hoping you'll sell it to me."

Color flooded his wind-scoured face. "Oh, no. I couldn't do that. You've already been so generous to me. Besides, it would be a mitzvah to give it to you," he said as he unpinned the fibula from the sash that hugged his belly.

The gold threw a glint of light onto the walkway as he handed it to me.

To quell the prick of tears, I closed the fist of my free hand and dug the fingernails into my palm.

"But will you tell me how you got it?" My voice, barely a whisper had taken on a hint of mischief.

Silence sat on the bench between us.

"Well," he said finally with a rueful smile, "I'm not so proud of that. So let me say I welcome this opportunity to make amends and ease the guilt that has taken up residence inside me like an unwelcome guest. I have no doubt the fibula belongs to you. A piece this elegant could belong to no one else, certainly not to Kastor."

"Kastor!"

"Yes, Zemirah, I stole it from him, and for that I am deeply ashamed. So you see, I'm hardly entitled to a reward from your uncle. And given that I can no longer ask Kastor for forgiveness, my only hope is that the Almighty will accept my contrition and restore me to grace for this belated attempt to make amends. Please don't think badly of me, but I sneaked into his room when he was out—"

"When was that?"

"Thursday afternoon. You remember how I jimmied his lock on Sunday, right? With my walking stick? I was so humiliated that morning when he shrieked his curses at me. I've sailed the seas my entire life, but never"—he rolled his lower lip over his upper one and shook his head, his eyes aimed at the ground—"never had I heard such profanity before. So I began to wonder whether he was hiding something, something valuable. And that's when—I can't deny it—a naughty curiosity took hold of me."

The island of sunlight shifted as a sea breeze tossed

the trees and flattened the spikes of the ripple grass.

"So, walking on tiptoes, I broke into his room. But all I saw was this one piece, the fibula, nothing more. I recognized the symbol for Roman citizenship engraved in the gold so I knew it couldn't belong to Kastor or anyone else staying here. And so I swiped it, for sheer spite, mind you, for no other reason. At the time, I wasn't afraid. I was too caught up in the drama of the moment. But as soon as I left his room and realized I had no way to re-lock his door, that he'd surely know I took it, I started to sweat even as my blood turned to ice. It's been only since he got killed that I've dared to wear it." Relief softened the lines in his weathered cheeks. "At least the Almighty has given me this opportunity to return it to you."

"That's so very kind of you, Mr. ben Ruben, for not only giving me the fibula, which is dear enough, but telling me how you got it." As I pinned it to my himation just below my right shoulder—Phoebe tells me that's where my mother wore it—I patted it and added, "Your secret is safe with me."

A smile of quiet satisfaction warmed his face.

"Now, if I could bother you with one more question."

He drew his brows together.

"Is there anything else you noticed in Kastor's room? I'm talking now about the things he might have had around."

"Well, he'd been working on a document. That's

when I realized he was a scribe, the supplies he had, the finest papyrus and ink, and needless to say, his penmanship was elegant. Again, I'm ashamed to admit it, but I was nosey enough to glance at it and see that it was a will. Of course, I didn't pay much attention beyond that. Once I'd taken the fibula, my guilty conscience chased me out of there faster than Bellerophon's ride on the stallion."

"And about your stick, Mr. ben Ruben."

He tightened his grip on the knob until his knuckles turned white.

"Could it have gone missing during that Thursday night before Kastor was killed? I mean, did you have it the next morning?"

"Ah, Zemirah!" he said, sighing deeply. "That's a long story. Yes, I stole that too, but only if that word applies to recovering my own goods from the very thief who'd taken them. Besides, this stick is not just any object, mind you. It's a part of me, the faithful friend that accompanies and even protects me." He loosened his grip and caressed it with prideful eyes. "So, needless to say, I noticed it was missing as soon as I woke up Friday morning, and yes, I figured Kastor had taken it to get even for the fibula. That's when I went to bang on his door—I was determined to have it out with him right then and there—and that's when I saw all that blood in the hall. It was early enough that I could have been the first one to notice it, and of course, I reported it immediately to Fabia, the only one around here with even the scent of authority.

"But I didn't take the stick then. I waited till everybody else knew he was dead. He had to be. All that blood and no answer, not even a moan when Fabia called to him. And mind you, with her pair of lungs! I knew if I ever wanted it back, I'd better grab it before the authorities came. But I didn't dare jimmy open his door, not with all the tenants standing around in the upstairs hall, shaking their heads at the river of blood, becoming fast friends with their estranged neighbors as they droned in sepulchral tones about how nice Kastor was, how smart he was, that he never bothered anybody—Ha!—pretending to be sad but really experiencing that peculiar blend of terror and relief. After all, even in this brutal world, murder still has the power to shock.

"So I went back to my room, pushed my trunk under the window, climbed up, and swiveled my head as I leaned out. Not a soul. It was broad daylight, mind you, but don't forget: Everybody was in the hall, aflame with curiosity, waiting to be questioned, the preferred alternative to being reported missing and then hunted down. So that's when I seized a tree branch, and moving hand over hand until I reached Kastor's window, I poked open the shutters and swung right in."

I marveled at not just the resonance of ben Ruben's voice but the coherence of his story and his choice of words, especially under the circumstances.

"I stayed but a minute, just long enough to snatch the stick. His room, of course, stunk worse than a butcher shop. Aside from the reek of death merging with the coppery odor of blood, the stench of his body wastes almost overwhelmed me. And then there was the sight of his battered corpse. But it was when I saw that my handsome stick had been the murder weapon—it had a few dents on the handle, a fresh gash, and was coated with a bloody slime—oh Zemirah, that's when I knew that along with snatching the stick, I was salvaging what was left of my humble life from the *summum supplicium*. The only trouble"—another deep sigh—"I forgot to pull the shutters closed behind me."

Beads of sweat pearled across his forehead. "Ah, but now I must go!" he said, his eyelids sagging. With no other postscript, he jumped off the bench, retrieved his bag, and listing from its heft, trudged toward the inn.

"Oh, please. I have just this one—"

I wanted to ask him why he waited until everyone knew Kastor was dead before sneaking into the dead man's room.

But my words sailed over the back of his head.

Oh, well. I'd found out that Kastor had stolen Amram's will. I still didn't know the connection between Kastor and my brother, but I was getting close. And I had the fibula. A chuckle floated out of my mouth as I imagined Binyamin's face when he saw me wearing it.

But that, I told myself, would have to wait until after the games.

# CHAPTER 16

*Wednesday afternoon, October 6th*:

Judah! Over here!" I said, waving my arms from a sliver of shade in front of the hippodrome.

"I see you, Miriam," he called, slipping through the throng with perfect grace.

He looked older in the mid-afternoon sunlight, the fine lines around his eyes etched more deeply, his springy mass of black curls still glossy but silvering at the temples.

I wanted to ask, "When, my darling, did age begin to leave its indelible mark on you?" But instead I asked, "What took you so long?"

"The Way was so congested that I couldn't get a chair—"

"Well, this is the first day, you know."

"Am I too late?" he asked, raking his hands through his hair.

"No, that would be impossible," I said, shaking my head in amusement. "The games are virtually endless, fifty bouts over four days straight, from early morning to sunset.

"We've missed the morning program, beginning with the *pompa*, that garish parade around the arena led by the *editor*, who, surrounded by his minions and wearing a purple toga and gilded, crown-like wreath, rides in a chariot drawn by exotic animals led by their trainers. Trailing that spectacle are the jugglers, dancers, acrobats, archers, and musicians, all wearing gold-embroidered cloaks, all throwing rose petals from their gaudy floats. Then, as the *noxii*, hunters, and finally the gladiators join the tail of the parade, the gladiators entering the arena through the *Porta Sanavivaria* (the Gate of Life), the cheers roll into one carnivorous roar that rises in pitch and volume as it swirls around the arena."

I remembered Binyamin telling me how, as a kid, he'd sneak into the games. As the parade came to a halt and the gladiators removed their armor, he'd thrill at the sight of them, their well-oiled athletic bodies glistening in the morning light while the young women, intoxicated by their own erotic fantasies, would moon over them, beckoning them with lewd gestures.

"And we've also missed the performing animals, wild beast hunts, and animal fights, probably even the *prolusio*, when the gladiators, accompanied by the shrill brass of trumpets and the mellow strains of the water organ, fight with wooden weapons to warm up. But don't worry; these acts are only the preliminaries. The main event, the gladiatorial combat, won't start till later this afternoon, and even then, I care only about Binyamin's bout—thankfully his last—which will be early in the afternoon program."

"Why early? I thought the best gladiators fight last."

"They do. But they're the younger, faster ones. Binyamin is older now, slower. Ordinarily, the *editor*, *lanista*, and the *doctores*—they do the pairing shortly before the games start—match combatants of equal ability to prevent the bouts from ending too swiftly. But in Binyamin's case, they'll match him with a *novus auctoratus*, probably one with little promise, so his victory is assured."

"I don't understand. Why would he be matched with a *novus auctoratus* rather than a *veteranus*?"

"According to Binyamin, the *editor* has to compensate the *lanista* for every gladiator killed. The higher the rank of the gladiator, the more the *editor* has to pay. Since Binyamin has reached the highest rank, the loss of his life would cost the *editor* too much, at least for the excitement the bout would generate."

Digging through my satchel, under the pouches of walnuts, amphorae of honey-sweetened water, and the seat cushions I'd brought for us, I groped for my leather purse and fished out the two *tesserae*, the coin-like disks of pottery I'd picked up at our branch of the Bank of Gabinius.

"Here," I said, pressing them into Judah's palm. "Show these to the usher. They're marked with our entrance gate, tier, sector, and seat numbers. "See," I said, tapping my index finger on the numerals. "Our seats are in the lower section of the third tier, which is reserved for upper class plebeians."

Although these tokens are free and good for the duration of the festival, you must have one to be admitted, and there're never enough to go around. I can still picture Papa when a messenger would knock at our door on route to delivering them to every adult male Roman citizen in the city. His nostrils flaring, his eyes glinting, and his spittle flying, my father would bellow in a gust of fury, "Get that filth out of here! We're Jews, not Romans!" And whenever the teenaged Binyamin would hear the echo of that indignation, he'd chase after the messenger to wheedle a *tessera* for himself and better yet, a few more to sell on the black market.

Bitterness and then resentment gripped me as I thought of my brother, who's flouted authority since infancy whether by guile, force, or some unerring combination of the two. Why did he have to absorb the blame for our mother's death and let the ensuing rejections, disappointments, and antagonisms drive him to the *ludus*? Why couldn't he feel a responsibility to contribute to our family's livelihood? Instead he seemed intent on draining our resources. Why did he have to trade his rights as a Roman citizen to become a social leper? Why couldn't he be more like other brothers, even Noah, who despite his meekness, was a loyal son intent on advancing his family's fortune and good name? And why was I here to watch this vulgar display of Roman power while Binyamin, contemptuous of even his own life, was willing to sacrifice his blood in this, the deadliest sport?

Judah may have noticed my jaw working, or perhaps he noticed me staring into space as if trying to decipher a message written there. I can say only that he interrupted my thoughts with a nudge and asked, "Miriam, are you ready to go inside?"

Turning to gaze at him, so composed, the sunlight curving over his cheekbones, bathing his face in a soft glow, I let go of my rage and was left instead with a hollow space and an acidic sorrow. I nodded.

And so, his palm between my shoulder blades, my feet inching forward, he steered me through the thousands milling about the ticket scalpers, souvenir hawkers, and sausage vendors who, from their covered stalls, seasoned the air with fennel and fried grease. As soldiers split the throng, we joined the stream of those funneling toward our gate, through an arch decorated with painted images of gladiators and charioteers in stucco relief. Judah checked the marble, wall-mounted diagram for the location of our seats and then directed me through an arcade to our stairway.

Before even climbing the steps, we caught the clack of wooden swords and the fits of raucous laughter springing from the antics of the *praegenarii*, the acrobatic dwarfs, cripples, and amputees who, accompanied by light-hearted music, amuse the crowd with their comic routines during intermissions. In tight-fitting costumes and outlandish plumed helmets, they exchange choreographed blows with their blunt weapons, lassoes, and nets to mock the gladiators.

As we located our row, crews of *arenarii*, the slaves who attend to the arena, were preparing for the standard gladiatorial bouts. Some were raking fresh, mica-flecked sand over the oysters of flesh and puddles of blood left on the field from the wild beast hunts. Others, to mask the sour smell of fear and the festering stench of death, were heating the aromatic cones from the stone pine trees planted around the hippodrome for that purpose. And a third crew was sprinkling the marble seats in the lower tiers with rosewater. Still nothing could neutralize the reek of misery rising through the wooden floor of the arena from the *hypogeum*. And nothing could fool the rats and the flies.

To claim our seats, we had to weave through the crush of sweaty bodies taking advantage of the break: the heavy-lidded spectators with worn shapeless faces, some restless, merely stretching their legs, others carving their way to the latrines; the roving food vendors with hardly an "excuse me" treading on everyone's toes as they peddled their honey-sweetened water and roasted lima beans; and the bookmakers, calling to their regulars as they jostled their way through the aisles, marking their tablets, and collecting the bets for upcoming bouts.

I unpacked the cushions, and by the time we settled into them, my satchel tucked between us, the tail of my himation fanned over my right shoulder, the *arenarii* had finished their tasks and the gladiators' swords were being checked for sharpness. A few minutes later, the wail of the double oboes interrupted the last clang of weaponry and signaled the start of the first bout.

ଓଃଓଃ

"So what are we seeing now?" Judah asked, his voice unnaturally loud to counter the thunderous music and the flapping of the *velarium*, the sailcloth awning that shades the spectators in the first three tiers. Sailors, recruited specifically to work its elaborate system of ropes and pulleys, were retracting the panels to welcome the late afternoon light.

"This first bout is between a *retiarius* and a *secutor*."

"So that must be your brother, the one without the helmet," he said, pointing to a vague spot in the air, his voice inflected more like a question than a statement.

"By the way, my brother's nom de guerre is Agrippa Fortitudo. And yes, he's a *retiarius*, but his bout is the next one."

"Are all the bouts today between a *retiar*—a what?"

"A *ret-eeeee-ar-eeeeeus* and a *se-cu-tor*. No, other kinds are on the program too, but this pairing is the most popular, its bouts the most exciting. Everyone says so many were trained in this weaponry because Claudius preferred watching a gladiator without a helmet. If the *retiarius* lost, Claudius could watch his face when his throat was cut. He didn't care whether the mob raised a forest of thumbs or whether its shouts of '*Mitte*!' or '*Missum*!' zigzagged from Rome to Capua and back. He'd order the execution just to gaze at the *retiarius*'s face in his death agony."

Judah shook his head in uneasy disbelief.

"Honestly, Judah, don't you remember anything from the games in Caesarea?" I teased, hoping a little banter would lighten our conversation.

A musical laugh bubbled out of him. "I remember your getting angry with me for ignoring you when in fact I thought I was doing what I was supposed to do."

"Excuses, excuses, excuses."

I welcomed the warmth of Judah's hand as he gave mine a quick squeeze. Then, in a comfortable silence, we bonded the way people do who are concentrating on the same spectacle.

But my needles of unease were also busy, their pricks less about this butchery or Binyamin's upcoming bout than his plans for the rest of his life. Did he still think he could buy the *ludus* here even though Sergius, who'd been sponsoring his dreams for years, refused to finance him? If not, then what else could he be planning?

I couldn't bear to think about it, but I couldn't resist thinking about it either. When I'd picture him employed, like many retired gladiators, as the bodyguard to a high-ranking politician, I'd recoil, knowing he'd be charged with assassinating the Roman's rivals. And so, as I forced myself to focus on the arena, I felt as if I were teetering on the lip of yet another vast pit, not just this one of freshly-raked sand but the pit into my own madness as well.

At that moment, the *secutor*, his left hand holding the shield vertically to protect most of his body, was warding off the repeated thrusts of the *retiarius*'s trident. He then tried to use his shield to strike a blow at the *retiarius*'s legs but was far too slow for his wily opponent. Instead the *retiarius* whirled around and circled the *secutor* to gauge the right moment to cast his net.

Binyamin had taught me that after a few dummy

lunges to test his opponent's vulnerabilities, the *retiarius*'s strategy is to snare his opponent with his net. But if the *retiarius* misses, the *secutor* might prevent him from snatching it back. Then he'd be left with only his trident and small dagger. And since most *retiarii* need both arms to control the heavy trident, they end up keeping the dagger tucked in their belt. Binyamin, however, strong enough to manage the trident with just one arm, can at the same time wield his dagger with the other, often to deflect the *secutor*'s sword or deliver the final blow, the only time he'd dare close in on his enemy.

When I looked again, the *retiarius* had caught the *secutor*'s sword between the points of his trident. Twisting the trident with both hands, he managed to wrench the sword out of the *secutor*'s hand.

From the notables in the first two tiers to the crush above us, the spectators, by then fiercely attentive, standing on their seats and brandishing their fists, erupted in a frenzied uproar, bellowing "*Habet*!" ("He's done for") or "*Hoc habet*!" ("Now he's had it!")

Moving back, lowering his trident as he transferred it to his right hand, the *retiarius* cast the net with his left, low enough to trip his opponent, who dropped to the sand like a felled ox. Then, as soon as the *retiarius* closed in, the hogtied *secutor* flung his shield and held up his arm, right index finger extended to signify his surrender and appeal for mercy.

The umpire rushed between them. Carrying a

wooden stick, prepared to use force to restrain the *retiarius*, he raised his arms to end the bout.

The gallery above us began to quake. The spectators, a sloping field of restless thumbs, shrieked "*Mitte*!" or "*Iugula*!" ("Slit his throat!"), depending on their loyalties and wagers.

The blasts from the pipe organ were lost in the hubbub. The umpire turned toward the *editor* for his verdict.

Suddenly, there was a tightly-coiled silence, the spectators spellbound, still as statues, anticipating the *editor*'s verdict. A palpable moment, and then a turn of his thumb.

The *secutor*'s life would be spared.

Strangers, becoming like family after sharing this life-or-death experience, thundered as one. Only a few shouted in disgust, "*Jugula, verbera, ure*!" ("Cut, beat, burn!") when the umpire let the *secutor* go.

A breath of relief from Judah and the fine lines around his eyes softened. For that moment, he looked young again.

Primal cheers accompanied the *retiarius* as the *editor* threw him a palm branch and a purse, which, according to Binyamin, would be no more than one-quarter of his market value, much of it destined for the *lanista*'s coffers. With a salute, the *retiarius*, flourishing his palm branch, bounded across the arena to exit through the *Porta Triumphalis* (the Gate of Triumph).

"Miriam, why did the spectators shout '*Iugula*' and then '*Jugula, verbera, ure*!'? Didn't your brother tell you they come for the showmanship, not the slaughter?"

"Well, maybe they felt the *secutor* didn't fight hard enough, that he didn't show enough *cupido victoriae*, what the Romans call the desire to win. Remember, instead of going bravely to his death, he begged for mercy. See, according to his oath, he's supposed to have contempt for death and be willing to die for the glory of Ro—"

"Shsh. You'll want to hear this."

The public crier was introducing the next pair of gladiators. I'd been talking so much that I missed the announcement about the *secutor* entirely and barely heard Binyamin's nom de guerre and record of recent victories. Even so, I was overwhelmed by such dread that I began to shiver despite the warmth of the afternoon sun.

Why? I couldn't say, only that I'd had that same premonition of calamity when I was racing toward Noah's house that Friday morning so long ago, that the three white-robed Fates were preparing me for a blow that in just a few minutes would stun me like a rock on impact and leave me gasping for breath.

ଓଓ

My eyes were on only Binyamin as he entered through the *Porta Sanavivaria* to rapturous applause. I saw the once-handsome face of the boy who'd dreamed of becoming a warrior. Here was my brother, my twin brother, the matchless athlete with the grace I always admired, the formidable competitor with the grandest ambitions, his gladiatorial career drawing to a close. And that afternoon, I also saw that Roman haughtiness in his eyes.

But before long, all eyes cocked toward the *secutor*, and the rapturous applause turned into a torrent of name-calling and taunts I'd never heard before. The spectators' rage was directed at Binyamin's opponent. The umpire was beating him with his stick to drive him toward the clearly marked ring in the center of the arena.

Who was this *secutor* who dared to defy the umpire's stick? Didn't he realize the assistant would come out next with the red-hot irons?

So I took a good look at him: his burly physique, thickset arms, and huge hands.

*Impossible! I must be going crazy. Dearest Almighty, tell me that my eyes are deceiving me.*

Because like a flash of lightning illuminating the night, I suddenly saw the underpinnings of a nefarious, multi-layered scheme, its monstrous deceptions and cold malignity.

"Idiot!" I howled, slapping my forehead.

"Miriam! What's the matter?"

My hand curled around my neck to stifle any more cries because I'd seen the *secutor*'s feet, sandaled in supple leather, the soles studded with hobnails, and the feet themselves like two enormous flatfish.

# Chapter 17

*Thursday Afternoon and Evening, October 7th*:

The sinking sun sent a shaft of orange light through the courtyard and onto my desk while a soft breeze sifting in from the peristyle rippled my tunic and tossed the ringlets at the nape of my neck. I'd been in my study all afternoon recovering the essence of the fern's leaflets from the dried waters, about to test the crystals for their solubility, when I heard Binyamin's unmistakable footfalls rounding the pool. But this time the soles of his *calcei* smacked the tiles with a listless rhythm.

Rubbing my aching neck, I looked up from my workbench—its furnaces, distilling pots, vessels, and retorts and its flasks of vinegar, urine, lemon juice, and vitriol—to watch him through the half-open doors as he trudged past, drunk and disheveled, wrapped in a chlamys splotched with a colorful blend of foul stains.

"Binny, we need to talk," I said in a flinty staccato I hardly recognized. His *rudis*, the wooden sword symbolizing the satisfaction of his contract with the *lanista*, was tucked under his right arm while with his left, he was making sluggish thrusts with an imaginary trident.

Turning toward me and wrinkling his face as if he smelled something bad, he answered with a few feverish blinks. Then, lumbering into my study, collapsing into the chair with his arms hanging down, he tilted his chin skyward and aimed his closed eyes at the ceiling.

I waited, expecting him to open his eyes and face me, but a silence closed in on us instead. Finally, I punched through the void. "What happened, Binny?"

Heavy-faced, he lowered his chin and held me with a blank stare.

"Binny, I need to know what happened to Tychon yesterday." My voice cut through the silence like a blade, sharper than I intended.

I could see the words forming in his throat, but he didn't speak.

And then, after another thick pause, he hissed a stream of curses that ended with his shrieking, "What's the matter with you? You were there, weren't you?"

I let the echo reproach me before I spoke again. "Yes, but I thought Tychon was scheduled to fight the day after you. You told me the two of you would never be paired. So what happened?"

"It happened."

"What do you mean 'it'?"

"Oh, can't you leave me alone?" he groaned while massaging his temples. "Since I came home, you haven't stopped picking on me, butting into my busi—Hey, hold on a minute." He'd been gazing at me with his world-weary eyes, but in an instant, his expression changed to a slit-eyed puzzlement and then, with a jolt that convulsed his entire face, he pointed at me with his chin. "What's that pinned to your tunic?"

"You mean this?" I asked as if I didn't know, making a singsong of my question while pointing to the fibula fastened to the right shoulder of my bodice. "Oh, that's right. You told me you had it, didn't you?" I tilted my head and pinned a wry smile on my face. "Hmmm. Yes, you told me that on Monday. I remember now." *As if I could ever forget*. "You said you hadn't unpacked it yet but you'd give it back to me after the bout."

"Oh, come on. Who are you kidding? By now you must know I lent it to Kastor until I could pay him with my purse—"

"Your purse!" I howled slamming my palm on the desk. Now my rage was in full bloom. "You never intended to pay him! You spent that purse a long time ago and more than once, I'll bet. You planned to kill him right from the start, didn't you?" I found myself goading him like Papa used to do.

"No, that's not true. But after Kastor was killed, I kind of lost track."

"Of the fibula."

"Yeah, the fibula." He'd started to gnaw on his upper lip, and then as he sucked it into his mouth, his eyes moved searchingly about the room from my cluttered workbench, to the drapes tied back behind me, and finally to the eyes of the asp, as if hoping each in turn would tell him how I got the fibula.

He shook his head.

"You mean Tychon couldn't find it," I prompted.

"Well, I just figured he took it."

"Took it from Kastor's room?"

"Yeah."

"Until you realized he wouldn't do that to you."

"Yeah. He was my friend, my real friend." He drawled the vowels in the word "real" to tell me he no longer regarded me as his friend.

And he was right. He just didn't yet know how right he'd be.

"So, why'd you kill your real friend?" I too drawled the vowels.

"Oh, Sis, it's such a long story." He drew in a miserable breath, and then, as his face twitched and his lips quivered, he rocked back and forth, his elbows on the desk, wringing his hands mindlessly.

I expected to see Tychon's blood caked under his fingernails.

As his wave of grief ebbed, he took a swipe at his eyes with the heels of his palms. Then folding his neck into a double chin, he dropped his head and murmured to his knees. "It wasn't supposed to end that way. Honest. Tonight we were supposed to splurge, you know, celebrate our discharge and new partnership at a really classy place. Remember you used to go to the Flamingo's Tongue with Phoebe? A place like that. And tomorrow we were gonna to try again to get sponsors for the *ludus*."

Binyamin never lost faith in his ability to bend the universe to his will.

"Poor guy, he didn't even know why he was in the arena. And then, when he recognized me, he refused to fight. And that's when the fans erupted in disgust, booing and shouting '*Jugula, verbera, ure*!'"

Binyamin pressed his fingertips against his lids, probably to shed that image. "So the *editor* had no choice. He gave the death verdict. Tychon must have known that would happen. That's when he knelt before me. Clasping my knees and bowing deeply, he bravely offered his neck while I slit his throat and he slumped to the sand. The spectators cried '*Habet*!' and it was all over."

At that moment, I realized my brother had become a

monstrous caricature of his former self, too dangerous to trust at large, and I was the only one to rein him in. Papa had tried and failed, and now it was up to me. So with an athletic readiness of my own, I lifted my shoulders in a prim upright position, angled my body to face him squarely—a sour sweat was washing his forehead—and summoned an uncommonly crisp and commanding voice:

"Binyamin, you have done a terrible thing, actually many terrible things, all intentionally, for your own gain. You are going to have to write all this down beginning with your plan to steal Amram's will. And it better be the truth, none of your usual swagger and lies."

Wrapping my arms around my chest, I prepared myself for an onslaught of resistance.

He scratched his head, his brows creased as if in disbelief. And then it came. "What are you talking about? None of this was my fault." And with a scowl, he added, "And who are you to tell me what to do anyway?"

His defiance was back, but it was milder than I expected.

"Besides, you know I can't write," he added shifting in his seat.

"Doesn't matter. Just write. Write as if you're talking to someone, as if you're explaining how it all happened, every detail."

"And if I don't?" he asked peevishly.

"Then I'll have to write up my own account and deliver it to the magistrate personally." I could see the consequences coiling through his conflicted brain until he raised his palms and nodded. "And I want it on my desk by Sunday morning."

Shaking his head, he struck the desktop and lurched to his feet while I wondered at the admiration and compassion I used to have for him. How I used to defer to him! Against my better judgment too! But how could I not? Papa was so arbitrary, so hard on my high-spirited brother. Except now I was left with a scream ringing through my soul that no amount of hot compresses and chamomile tea could relieve.

# Part 2
# Binyamin's Story

"Hope of ill gain is the beginning of loss."
~ Democritus

# CHAPTER 18

My sister is making me write this, in case it's any of your business, which, unless you're a magistrate and I fail to live up to my agreement with her, it isn't. She said, "Put it all down. You know what'll happen if you don't." So I'm doing what she said because you know my sister. And yeah, I'm telling you I'm not good at this writing stuff—not like her, who's good at everything, at least that's what people think—but here goes anyway.

I'm gonna start this story with my becoming a gladiator. I left Alexandria for Capua ten years ago, when I was sixteen, full of the hopes and dreams of every young man, ready to satisfy the blood lust of the Empire and fight with the desperation that attended my growing up in a family where I was the outsider, where nothing I did was ever right. But I'm not gonna bore you with all that. By now you know I killed my mother, right? And let's not forget Titus, who, to tell you the truth, was a jerky kid anyway.

I hoped to prove my worth as a first-rate gladiator, as a *primus palus* in my *familia gladiatoria.* That means belonging to the highest of the four gladiatorial ranks based on the number of my bouts and victories, an achievement something like being the senior centurion of a legion if you know anything about the Imperial Roman Army. But most of all, aside from getting away from Papa, who was a tyrant if ever there was one, I dreamed of being awarded the *corona*. That's the laurel wreath, the ultimate award for an exceptional bout, which, along with my other accomplishments in the arena, would be engraved on my tombstone. Not that anyone would care, certainly not my sister.

Anyway, I loved the challenge, the fear, and the accolades. In the arena, I felt alive for the first time, something none of the women I've ever known could do for me.

# CHAPTER 19

And it was at the *ludus* in Capua, that I met Tychon, the best and only friend I ever had. I'll tell you more about him soon enough, but first I'm supposed to tell you how I hatched the plan to have Kastor borrow Amram's will and write me in as the principal beneficiary. Oh, and along with that, he was supposed to add a few lines about how I was like a second son to Amram, the son he secretly wanted, a man of action, rather than the sissy he got stuck with, who, with his apologetic perspiration, would toady to my father all the time.

I knew Kastor would do it. He hated my sister like poison, my father too, for selling him to the civil authorities.

"For no reason at all," he said.

Did he really think I'd believe that? Of course, my father was already dead so Kastor couldn't settle the score with him, but I knew he'd want to get even with my sister. Besides, I promised Kastor a cut of the inheritance and gave him my mother's fibula as collateral, which frankly was all I had left to give him.

Sorry about that, Sis.

Okay, so where was the harm? That old jaundiced Amram had so much money and no heirs, except my sister, who, when that foul-smelling boyfriend of hers died, ingratiated herself to the hilt with his wisp of a father. Anyway, she'd only have given that money away. You think I'm kidding? Go ask her yourself.

*But if she thinks I planned to kill the old geezer, she's wrong, dead wrong. Okay, so I just made a little joke. My sister will probably make me scratch it out. She barges into my room all the time now, probably to make sure I haven't jumped out the window like I used to do when Papa would ground me. But no, I realize I have to write this. What I mean is I know what she'll do to me if I don't.*

Amram himself gave me the idea about the will when I saw him that first Friday night I was in Alexandria. A fleshless, yellow-skinned mummy, he was panting and wheezing like he'd put up a good fight but was no match for Charon, who'd been trying to herd him onto the Ferry with all the other sinners. So you see, I had no need to kill Amram. I knew I wouldn't have long to wait for the money, and besides, I still thought I could count on my dear sister—my very own twin sister mind you, sitting on her very own throne of money—to help me buy our dinky *ludus* in Alexandria.

I realized afterward I was stupid to approach her on Shabbat, especially when I saw the skin tighten over her jaw. But I could also tell she'd never finance my project, no matter how or when I'd ask, even if I had a million other investors and needed only one paltry drachma, which is worth about five liters of wheat, in case you keep track of that stuff the way my sister does. And like I told her, which I knew would be a waste of breath, she'd become just like Papa, against anything and everything I ever wanted.

Okay, so I gave her time to think it over, figured it wouldn't hurt to ask again, but the next day, sure enough, she called my enterprise "shadowy" if you can imagine that and gave me what amounted to a flat refusal. Only then did I go to the Public Records Office to see Kastor. And like I said, he was eager to make the deal, very eager. Honestly, he practically suggested it. And just think that poor bastard could've bought his freedom with his share of my windfall. Who knows? He could've been fired for plotting to steal that kind of money from my pigheaded father. Hey, I would've tried the same thing.

"No problem," he said, rubbing his greedy palms together. "I can take the will out of Amram's box tomorrow, match the ink, sealing wax, and stationery—"

Was he a professional, or what! I never even thought of the matching part.

"—and have it done in no time. But look, I'm taking a chance here with my job and all, not much, but still I'm going to need some collateral, something up front—"

"Yeah, yeah. I follow. Come to the house tomorrow, and I'll give you something to secure the deal."

To tell you the truth, I didn't want to be seen anywhere with that skulking jackal, certainly not at the Public Records Office while all this was going on. What business would people think I could possibly be having with him there or, come to think of it, anywhere else?

You know what I mean? And I certainly didn't want to go to his place. I'd been to enough greasy *cellae* looking for cheap whores and dice games to last a lifetime.

So I told him to come to the house that following afternoon. I knew Miriam would be out meeting with some perfume maker. And you know what? I had a good laugh sitting in the big chair, my feet on the desk, taking possession of the study like I was a big-shot banker or something because I knew if Papa could see me, he'd groan louder than all the *noxii* caged in the *hypogeum*.

So I gave Kastor the fibula and a drachma or two for the stationery, and then I hustled him out the door faster than Mercury can fly. Anyway, that's how it all got started.

# CHAPTER 20

Like I said, that's how it all got started. But soon enough—must have been Wednesday, probably early afternoon because I was still sleeping—a chain of rants echoed through the house, slapping my eardrums. It was Gershon, a parasite if I ever saw one, bringing his upper-crust stink into the house. He was bawling something about the Fates and then that the will was missing. *Of course, the will was missing*, I said to myself, but a moment later, my eyes flew open, and I realized *only Kastor and I should know that*. And that's when my brilliant plan began to fall apart, like a spider web one strand at a time, all because of that meddler. Well, I jumped into my clothes and scurried over to Kastor's *cella* in the western end of the *Bruchium* quarter, the last place in this dung-smeared world I wanted to be.

I don't have to tell you about the neighborhood. We all know what garbage, urine, and cheap wine smell like. Besides, I'm trying to get on with what my highfalutin sister calls my account of events. I managed to find his building easily enough, the ugliest tenement on a block of five-story, run-down dwellings, his with an exterior staircase zigzagging to the roof.

I clambered up the steep, narrow stairs two at a time to the fifth floor, the steps scuffed and bowed by years of neglect, and poking open a low, flimsy door, ducked my head and strode in. He was sitting hunched over a table in front of a slit-like window, a *calamus* in his hand, an inkwell, sheets of papyrus, and a sharpening knife within easy reach.

The sour-onion stink of his sweat and whatever he'd had for lunch grabbed me by the throat.

"Hey, what's new, partner?" he asked, looking up. Scraping the legs of his chair against the sagging floor boards, he pushed away from the table and brought his stink right to my nose.

"We have a little problem." I announced. Stepping back, I leaned against the door jamb, my arms locked across my chest.

"Oh yeah?" He plunked down his pen at the same time his eyebrows shot up, like he was a marionette with all the strings connected.

"Yeah. Someone noticed the will is missing from

Amram's box, which means everyone knows it by now."

"How in Hades did that happ—"

"Never mind. Can you finish it and get it back today before my sister can verify it's missing? I mean like right now."

"You must be kidding!" An indignant tone had crept into his voice. "I've taken the scroll apart and re-written some of the panels, but I'm hardly half way. We're talking a couple more days, at least."

"What? You said it would take no time. I took you at your word." By then, I was practically screaming. *Who did that snake think he was, using that tone with me?*

"Besides, you have to get me the old man's seal ring before I can complete the—"

"His what?"

"Let me fini—"

"I don't even know where that is, never mind how I'm gonna get it."

"Didn't I tell you I have to match the sealing wax? What did you think I meant?"

Then, after shaking his head in disbelief, he lowered his voice to a thin whine. "Look, I'm the one in danger here. Amram's a Roman citizen. There'll be an investigation. Your priggish sister will see to that. And you know how that story will end. You've got to get me on a ship out of here tomorrow."

"Are you crazy?" At that point, I was the one shaking my head. "It's the end of the month. Nothing's moving in these harbors." My voice was laced with spite. Still I enjoyed watching the fear engulf him, his wild eyes staring and his mouth falling open, a blank look of terror on his now-pasty face.

"Then you've got to hide me until I can book passage somewhere, anywhere, even Cyprus." he was stuttering and sputtering by then, spraying me with bits of sound. "Surely a ship could reach there before the end of the season."

Shows how much he knew! Even you probably know that any ship heading north would be sailing into the teeth of the Etesians. Only a Roman naval vessel would dare challenge those winds and only to haul critical cargo or transport troops. Squads of oarsmen would have to beat the choppy sea while the swells fought back, smashing the deck with sheets of their rage. But I wasn't going to convince that milksop of anything.

"Okay, okay. Just stop your whining. I know an inn on the waterfront. I can get you in tonight. Stay put. I'll be back."

When I left, he kept muttering, "Where is *Dolos* when I need him?" whoever he is, while he pounded the table with his fists.

# CHAPTER 21

As wild as it sounds now, I still had hope that Kastor would finish the will so I could stash it in Amram's house where someone would find it, especially if I could count on a little help from Leo, that new, moon-faced manservant. So, after making arrangements with a certain naughty *cauponaria* at The Pegasus—I charged it all on Sergius's tab—I sent a message with her porter to Kastor that he could come on over and settle in. Then I hung around, had a few drinks with Tychon until the night thickened enough for me to sneak into Miriam's study and search for that lousy seal ring.

Now you're not gonna believe this, but when Kastor arrived and I introduced him to my good buddy, that whining ingrate pulled me aside and scolded me for not delivering the message to him personally.

"What's the matter with you?" he hissed, adding a stream of curses I won't even bother to mention. My sister would only make me scratch them out anyway. "See what you've done! I can't go back to the Public Records Office now. You've set me up for a capital offense." Going on and on, his features convulsed, he jerked his head in the direction of the porter and finished with, "Now he can identify me."

*Well, if he couldn't before, he certainly can now.*

Look, I patiently listened to his sniveling, tilting my head to the side, my lips pursed, my arms folded across my chest while the fury ripped through me. I wanted to strangle him right then and there, crush his windpipe with my bare hands just to see those wild eyes pop out of his head. I'd had enough of his skittishness not to mention his impudence. And why was he blaming me when it was all that lily-livered meddler's fault anyway?

Okay. So where was I? Oh, yeah. The search for the ring. I'll get to that soon enough, but first I gotta tell you I left the inn with fear howling through my belly. Even now, my penmanship turns spidery as my memory hurls me back to that night, and I shake my head in disbelief.

I wasn't even thinking about how Kastor would book passage let alone secure an exit visa. I was thinking about what would happen if the authorities pinch him before he can board a ship out of here. By tomorrow, when their slave fails to show up for work, they'll comb the city, first checking his *cella* and then the inns along the waterfront. And since they can't recoup their investment by selling him to a *ludus*—his clubfoot, remember?—they'll sentence him to *damnatio ad bestias*. And when he's pleading for his life, he'll implicate me. That was the fear consuming me.

So, by the time I got to my sister's study, I realized I'd probably never get to use the seal anyway. Still I gave the room a cursory search.

You know, I don't even know whether I've already written this. My sister has me so befuddled. Of course, she'd blame it on my drinking, the only thing that gives me any peace around here. Nothing is ever her fault. Well, never mind. If I wrote it already, that's too bad. Like I said, I'm no Homer.

Anyway, the desk was clear of everything except that glass oil lamp, the one that used to give me the shivers. That asp's gaze was as powerful as a glance from the deadly basilisk. I was certain it could read my mind and see through my every lie. But her workbench was cluttered with vessels and flasks and Jupiter knows what else. Oh yeah, and a row of metal chunks, some silver, some gold, but odd shapes and sizes. What she could be doing with all those nuggets I hadn't a clue, but I wouldn't put anything past her. And if I thought I could have gotten away with it, I'd have taken the larger pieces for all the trouble she was putting me through.

I groped inside the baskets on her shelves, but they contained only *calami*, bottles of ink, half-used sticks of sealing wax, and some sheets of papyrus. I didn't bother upending the furniture or riffling through the ledgers. I knew that was pointless. She had no reason to hide that thing.

So, yeah. Another strand of the web had fallen apart, but I hardly cared anymore. I knew I had to shut Kastor's mouth. I just didn't know how I was gonna do it, not then anyway.

# CHAPTER 22

So back I went to The Pegasus the next afternoon. And that's when Tychon gave me an earful. And I'll bet you can guess what it was about.

"As soon as you left for home last night, Kastor singled out this potbellied dwarf, not a bad guy you understand, a harmless itinerant, and started a row with him."

"About what?"

"Nothing that makes any sense. But then this morning, it really got out of hand. Just ask the counterman."

See what I mean? Kastor really needed someone to shut his mouth before Fabia herself called the authorities. Believe me, she knows everybody. If she weren't so ugly, you'd say she must be sleeping with Nero himself or at least a couple of his magistrates. That's the way she is. So Tychon and I worked out a plan to help Kastor, well, more to help ourselves but for Kastor's own good anyway.

See, nothing's as bad as *damnatio ad bestias*. First the frenzied beasts bound into the arena as if on springs. There you are, bound to a stake, looking into their open jaws, their yellow fangs and purple tongues covered in froth. You hear their savage howls. Then you inhale what must be unimaginable pain while they, standing on their hind legs, devour chunks of your flesh in a widening mist of blood and flies. Can you imagine that? And, I assure you, that would've been his sentence.

But look, before I get too far along in my account, the one my dear sister—did I mention yet that she's my *twin* sister?—so generously offered me the opportunity to write. Ha! I guess I have to tell you what happened that night. Okay. Thursday. Yeah, Thursday night. Tychon and I went to that cookshop near the canal, the one where Sergius hangs out. It wasn't exactly a social call, but I figured, hey, after all he's done for me, it's only right I offer him a piece of my *ludus*.

He was ripe for the action, of course, his swollen eyes keen with excitement—which only made that weepy discharge of his trickle even faster—but he was a little short of cash like the rest of us. So, I had to disappoint him. I can't go around cutting everybody a share unless they buy in, right? Even my sister would agree with that.

And then, just as I finished writing about my sister agreeing—and this is really weird—she sashays into my suite, leans over my shoulder like I was a kid and she was my tutor or something, and reads what I wrote about Sergius.

"Binyamin, when I offered you the opportunity to write your account of what happened, you agreed to tell the truth. Unvarnished. No swagger and no lies."

"Well, what do you think I'm doing here, writing *The Diliad*?" At that moment, I felt as if she'd struck me. With that rage coiling inside me, I stood and swiveled around to face her.

*Yes, Sis, I'm gonna write all this down, even the parts about you. You asked for the unvarnished truth, and now you're gonna get it, every bit of it.*

Hey, if she were a man, I'd have wrestled her to the ground right then and there like I did to Titus and wonder why I hadn't done it sooner. But to tell you the truth, I realized years back when I refused her offer in Caesarea that she never understood me. She wanted to use her share of our mother's jewelry to buy out the contract with my *lanista*, remember? So I could crawl back home to her and Papa. No kidding.

Now you can see why I brought Tychon home with me, to have someone I could count on. He could have traveled with the rest of the troupe, you know. And you wanna know what else? I knew she wouldn't like him, and I was glad! So what does she want from me now? I'm doing everything she told me to do. Besides, she didn't exactly offer me this opportunity. She had me boxed into a corner, and she knew it.

"You need to state right here and now how you and Tychon planned to *protect* Kastor from *damnatio ad bestias*." She said the word "protect" as if it dirtied her mouth. At the same time, she pointed with her faintly quivering index finger at my manuscript. "Or our deal is off." Then she swallowed twice to clean her mouth.

"Okay," I muttered to the floor as she flounced out of my suite.

# CHAPTER 23

So here's what I have to say about our plan to protect Kastor. Tychon and I—really Tychon—he saw how uncontrollable Kastor had become—hatched the plot while we were heading over to see Sergius. And I went along with it. After all, wasn't it only logical that Tychon should be the one to solve Kastor's problem since they both were rooming at The Pegasus practically in each other's lap? And wouldn't everybody at The Pegasus think it was the dwarf, who obviously had a motive to kill Kastor? Or maybe Fabia and her counterman, if they had any spine. And wasn't it Tychon who'd already had experience staging an ambush?

My sister may tell you about Tychon strangling that tax collector in Caesarea, not that she'd ever see Tychon as justified. For all I know, she'd say Tychon killed Arrius Corvus to steal the money he'd squeezed out of the boy's father and was angry the tax collector had gotten so little. Ha! Anyway, where was I? Oh, yeah, the plan.

So Tychon climbed in through the window—in broad daylight, mind you, no doubt startling Kastor. Of course, Kastor was no match. Oh, he put up a good fight all right, even with that clumsy foot of his. Well, why not? He was fighting for his life. Besides, these scrawny guys have an agility that can really surprise you. I've seen it in the arena hundreds of times. But remember, Tychon was a professional. He was used to fighting under the weight of forty pounds of armor.

He'd planned to strangle Kastor with his bare hands like he did the tax collector, but then, spotting the walking stick, he figured why not implicate the dwarf while he was at it? So my good buddy bashed in Kastor's skull with the dwarf's stick. Perfect! After all, the dwarf could never have reached Kastor's neck, but with the stick, he could even have reached Kastor's head. I'm telling you, I still laugh whenever I think about it.

And then Tychon took the will and the copy—by the way, I took great pleasure burning them on Shabbat—and dove out the window, hooked onto a branch, and swung back into his room. Too bad he couldn't find the fibula though. I figured he just took it as a souvenir. Hey, why not? I'd have done the same thing.

# Chapter 24

The last strand of the web fell away on the Sunday night after Kastor's death. Tychon and I were trailing a bunch of rowdy sailors through the twisting lanes around the *Kibotos*, hoping they'd lead us to a dice game where Fortuna would favor us. I inhaled deeply to free my nose from the stench of the canal only to smell my companion's breath, sour and pungent, as if he'd puked up his supper.

"Everything okay, good buddy?"

When he turned to answer, the light from a half-open door gathered in the fresh lines pinching his brow.

"Don't know."

"Don't know what?"

He heaved a sigh. "Your sister. She has a friend at The Pegasus."

"What are you talking about?"

"She visited him this afternoon."

"*Merda*!"

And just then—can you believe it?—this mangy cat skulks out of an alley. I kicked it in the belly so hard it flew with a squeal you could hear all the way to Pharos Island, exactly the way I would have liked to kick my sister.

"Hey, what's with the cat?"

I glared at him in silence while that very question buzzed through my own head, but as my reason trickled back, I answered with a question of my own. "So tell me, what was Miss Busybody doing there?"

"Somehow she hooked up with that dwarf, they got a little cozy, you know, whispering, giggling, and all that, and then he led her up to his room."

I knew what he was thinking, and I know what you're thinking, but you're as flat out wrong as he was.

"No way," I said, folding my arms and shaking my head vigorously. "My sister doesn't do that kind of thing. She wouldn't have gone upstairs unless she thought—" *Oh Jupiter, unless she thought she could learn something about Amram's will or—oh, no!—about Kastor's murder!*

So there we were blinking at each other in an expanding panic, my teeth clenched, his face white to the lips. I snatched a few quick breaths for courage while he gnawed on a jagged cuticle and sucked out the blood.

Look, I know this sounds lame, but I'm no match for my sister's guile and that goes double for Tychon. So I had to face it. Like it or not, I was gonna have to get Albus, our trainer, to pair me in the arena with Tychon instead of the clod they were bound to match me up with. Oh yeah, and Albus would have to drug my buddy's *sagina* the morning of the bout. See, I began to figure out a plan right then and there. Poor Tychon, he was just too slow-witted to hold up against my sister's grilling. And that was gonna be bad to boot because I knew I'd miss him, you know? He was as loyal as an old dog but sad to say, just as dense. Before he realized it, he'd be turning us both into lion fodder.

And you know how I got Albus to do it? Come on, take a guess. I pledged my purse and bonus for winning the match. Oh yeah, I'd already borrowed against them, but he didn't know that. Hey, you can't blame a guy for trying, right? And then to clinch the deal, I promised him the top job in my *ludus*, the one I'd have given Tychon had our plan worked out, namely head of the dozen or more *doctores* I was gonna hire.

Anyway, I'm sure my bout wasn't the first one Albus ever fixed. Ha!

Of course, my sister probably had everything figured out as soon as she saw the umpire beating Tychon. So that's why I'm writing this *megillah*: because my sister is too smart for her own good. But don't forget that nosey blabbermouth Gershon, that greedy vulture Albus, and of course, Kastor, a coward if there ever was one. The whole stinking lot of them only proves what I've always said: You can't trust anybody.

Written and sealed in fulfillment of the agreement with my sister, Miriam bat Isaac,

Βινψαμιν βεν Ισααχ

The seal of Binyamin ben Isaac

Alexandria *ad Aegyptum*

October of the Second Year of the Reign of Nero Claudius Caesar Augustus Germanicus

# PART 3
# MIRIAM'S STORY

"Acquittal of the guilty damns the judge."

~ Horace

# CHAPTER 25

*Monday Afternoon, October 11th*:

Binyamin bounded into my study, his feet barely touching the floor, his tone too loud and his words too fast. He was like a well-oiled politician except his verbena hardly masked his sour breath and last night's cheap wine.

"So, can I have my manuscript back now, my unvarnished, true account, without my usual swagger and lies?" His sarcasm was in full bloom as he stood before me, casting a withering glance at me as I looked up from my desk. His feet stood apart authoritatively, but his face was haggard as if he were carrying ten more years than when he first came home. Leaning in close, flecks of froth collecting on his lips, he spoke in a burble of slurred syllables.

"Surely you've read it, probably stayed up last night to finish it, if I know my sister. I'm no Homer, but how'd I do?"

"I'm keeping it."

His body stiffened inside his long, loosely wrapped, silk robe while a crease deepened across his forehead.

"Whatever for?"

"Because our business isn't finished yet."

"Look, I did what you wanted." Astounded, he dropped his eyes, turned his palms outward, and asked, "Now what?"

"Did you really think writing an account of what happened to Kastor and Tychon would absolve you from any further consequences?"

As if perplexed, he stepped back with narrowed eyes. "You said if I did that, you wouldn't report me to the magistrate. So I broke a few rules. Big deal. Everyone does, especially the magistrates." His wicked mouth loosened into a false, overly hearty, wine-logged laugh, which he chopped off abruptly as soon as my eyes ensnared his. "Besides, you yourself said Kastor was a complainer—"

"I also said his death should be avenged."

His jaw hinged open.

"Okay, Sis, so what did you have in mind? You want me to run around the block a few times?"

The time had come to tell him.

Remembering my struggle last night with the sleep that wouldn't come, I drew in a careful breath.

ᘓᘓ

I'd read Binyamin's account last evening in the meager circle of light flickering from Papa's precious oil lamp. Then later, in my *cubiculum* as I lay tossing on my sleeping couch, I brooded over my decision even as the darkness paled to an early-morning gray. I tried to balance the depravity of his acts with his righteous deeds as a boy, but they were too few to tip the scales.

As a boy, Binyamin was simply naughty. He'd rush the mule carts as they clattered over the pavement, vault over their tailgates, and toss handfuls of fodder from the driver's scuttle into the street or worse yet, at the beggars, street philosophers, and soothsayers lining the Way. He'd stay too long at the beach, tunneling under the waves, slicing through the foam, or challenging the breakers until our maid had to send for Papa's bodyguard to fish him out. Ordinarily he'd resist going to the synagogue, but occasionally he'd join us so he could tease the bashful girls and chase them around the sanctuary in and out of every set of bejeweled doors when they tried to escape from him. And he'd cut geometry class or skip school entirely not so much to savor his freedom as to spite Papa, who refused to send him to a *collegium iuvenum*.

Binyamin was also rebellious. When he'd be grounded, he'd sneak off to the games to admire the broad-shouldered masculinity of the gladiators or jump out his window bound for Zenon's cook-shop, where he'd gamble or relieve his lust in the pantry with the proprietor's voluptuous daughter.

And all the while, I'd be his alibi. "No, Papa, that couldn't have been Binyamin swiping fruit from the produce stand—" *After a juggling act that culminated in his tossing the vendor's pomegranates to a ring of adoring ragamuffins.* "—or filching candy from Apollon's *pantopoleion*—" *Confections that he easily could have paid for.* "—we were studying geometry in my suite all evening. Honest, Papa."

In exchange, Binyamin would teach me how to stand on my head, shinny up a tree, or take aim at a snake with his slingshot. And he'd coach me in boxing, showing me how to estimate my opponent's reach; maintain my footing on sand; and throw, duck, and even take a punch. Still, no matter how hard I tried, I could never outfox him, outrun him, or outmaneuver him.

So, on that Monday morning, recalling his boyhood antics, I lay weary but wakeful as the darkness paled and the first glints of sunrise found their way into my *cubiculum* and prodded my gritty eyes open. I wished Phoebe were here with me, her pallet next to my sleeping couch, comforting me as she used to by cradling me in her arms, subduing me with her coos, and catching my tears in a fragrant linen square before they could sting my face like beads of vitriol.

Rather than continue tossing restlessly, cringing from the blurry images that battered me, dwelling on how as youngsters, I'd enabled my brother's waywardness, I donned a short, sleeveless tunic and padded to my study to re-read his account. I'd hoped for a different version of the events, but the second reading only confirmed my decision about his future. And so I gathered the sheets of papyrus together and laid them on my workbench.

ઌઌ

Drawing in another careful breath, this time with my common sense controlling my imagination, I cleared my throat to tell him my decision.

"Binny, you need to go back to the *ludus*."

My voice, cold and flat, soaked up all the air in the study.

His lips fell open, and his eyes went wide with shock.

"I what?"

"You heard me."

"Wait a minute! The ships aren't even sailing anymore, unless you think I can disguise myself as a government official and board a war galley."

"No," I said, ignoring his sarcasm and rising from the chair. "I understand it's too late in the season for you to get back to Capua. I meant for you to join the *familia gladiatoria* here, at the *ludus* in Alexandria."

His muscles hardening, he lengthened his neck. "Are you crazy?" he snapped. "I'm not going to fight for this dinky *ludus*. I want to establish my own, a *ludus* Alexandria can be proud of. And I intend to raise the money myself among the fans here. You saw them. Day after day, the hippodrome packed. And you heard the raves. I depended on my family to raise the money—not a great idea, I admit—but I realize now I can reach out to aficionados like Gershon, who love the games."

He heaved a sigh and then continued in a grief-clogged voice that sounded as if it had come through the labyrinth of tunnels that brought us our water from the Nile.

"Besides, Miriam, I'm too old. You should see the young talent. I wouldn't last in the arena a year, never mind five. For me to sign another contract with any *ludus* would be a death senten—"

He'd been pacing back and forth in front of my desk, his arms pawing the air as he spoke. But then, having advanced into the courtyard, his long pearly shadow streaming backward toward me, he suddenly whirled around, his silk robe rustling with fury, his pupils dilated, his face twisted into a snarl.

I could feel the pulse of my own fear creeping up my neck.

"Ooooh, I get it. Finally," he said nodding, pinching

his lips and tapping his brow with an index finger. "This is how you planned to get rid of me all along, isn't it? So you could keep all this for yourself." Swiveling his head, he swept the study with an expansive arm. "Send him back to the *lud*—"

"No, I see this as a way for you to start over, do penance for your crimes, get your debts forgiven, and build on your legend—"

"And when I'm slain—because that's inevitable, you know—and 'Charon' has tested me with his red-hot iron, the *libitinarii* will carry me off to the *spoliarium* like any other piece of flesh."

The *spoliarium*! Oh my Lord! His mention of that pit plunged me back to Caesarea and that gruesome chamber under the arena, its indescribable stench, its dim patches of cold light, the squeals of its scrabbling rats, and the din of its slaves salvaging the armor and weaponry from the rows upon rows of corpses stacked clear to the ceiling!

I wondered whether Binyamin saw that flicker of alarm in my eyes.

"Or maybe I never told you," he added. "The *lanistae* say the slaves prepare the bodies for mass burial there. What a joke! You think they'd waste all that fresh meat? They cut us up and feed us to the lions to whet their appetite for human flesh."

I pulled in a breath to quell my revulsion and strengthen my resolve. "No. I will buy back your body and provide a funeral for you, a magnificent memorial with an honorable burial and later an everlasting monument with your name and record as an outstanding gladiator."

"Right! You really expect me to believe that? Ha!" He wiped a string of spittle from his mouth with the back of his hand. "Just like Papa, you've opposed everything I've ever wanted, but at least he did so openly."

I could smell his sick, sour wine-breath and see the bitterness in his eyes. "I think you should sit down now, Binny."

"And you know what? You're a sneak, a filthy, rotten, two-faced sneak. And you enjoy being one. Even when you were betrothed to Noah, you'd sneak over to Judah's shop whenever you got the chanc—"

"Please Binny, let's both sit down."

He'd begun to move around the desk toward me, hemming me in against my workbench, slapping me with a wicked smile when he recognized his handwriting on the sheets of papyrus I'd laid on the workbench.

"I want my manuscript back, and I want it now," he brayed.

"I can't give it to you."

"Even if I'm willing to settle down and help you run the family business?"

"Not now and not ever."

"Then I'll have to take it from you."

"No, you really won't, Binny. Your confession is safe with me as long as you join the *ludus*."

He ignored me and glanced around. "I'm not going to join that *ludus*. I'm going to *buy* it." His words reverberated inside my chest. "You know, if I have to, I'll kill you for it."

A shiver bounced through me, despite the scalding rivulets of sweat trickling down my spine. But his threat only reinforced my determination.

He reached inside his robe, drew out an ivory-handled short dagger, probably the one he used in the arena, and pointed it at my face.

The afternoon sun caught the blade.

I let out a gasp.

That's when I set my feet firmly astride, one foot forward, the other angled just as he'd taught me.

Likewise, he stood perfectly still, leaning forward, his legs apart, his knees soft, his eyes ablaze once again with the thrill of the arena.

"You learned your lessons well, but I'm going to kill you anyway." He brandished his dagger. "Do you know how many I've butchered with this?"

He broke into a savage whoop of malicious laughter, the terrifying howl of an unsound mind, part strangled sob, part high-pitched wail.

Carving the air, he trained his gaze on me.

He moved forward.

I thought of my narrow escape from the assassin's dagger in Caesarea and stepped back against the drapes. My palms rose, as if they could ward him off.

He closed the gap.

I knew he could kill me. For now, though, he seemed to be enjoying the game too much.

But I was tiring, the seconds lengthening. I needed to get this over with. “No, I don’t know how many, but I do know you ripped out the innards of our dear mother, that saintly soul who wanted only to give you life—”

That was when he charged.

I drove my fist into his jaw just below the left ear and felt the pain all the way to my shoulder. He smashed me back with bone-crushing force. My head snapped sideways. My left cheekbone caught fire.

The floor swayed.

He smiled triumphantly. And then he plunged the dagger into my right shoulder. A warm wetness spread across my chest. He should have stabbed me on the left side. He must have wanted to prolong his amusement.

“I’m going to kill you slowly,” he said as if reading my mind.

I felt the heat but not the pain. At first. Then its sharpness burst inside me, and I felt myself getting dizzy.

But I braced myself and reached for a flask. Any flask. The vitriol. And I watched his feet. When he rushed toward me, I hurled the contents. His eyes widened, and he yelped in pain.

I’d tried to aim for his chest—I couldn’t bear to disfigure that once-handsome face—but some of the acid must have splashed onto his mouth because a brown, gelatinous mucus began to ooze from his lips.

He skittered backward, clawing the air, crashing to the floor. His face hardened into a mask of rage.

The last I'd see of him in this world.

"Solon! Orestes!"

I heard my mouth blurt out a string of orders: Solon to chain Binyamin, rinse him in the pool, and then fetch Sergius. Orestes to bring me Amram's triangular-faced physician, the one adept with ligatures, to staunch my bleeding. With that, I left behind the murderous scream in my shoulder to slip into a blissful darkness.

# The Fifth Year of the Reign of Nero Claudius Caesar Augustus Germanicus (Nero) 59 CE

"As you have sown, so shall you reap."

~ Cicero

# EPILOGUE

*Monday Afternoon, September 17th*:

So now you know why I've been obsessing these past three years over how my life might have been different had Binyamin fought his last bout elsewhere, perhaps never coming back to Alexandria at all. Then he wouldn't have encountered Amram on that Shabbat evening, fleshless and bloodless as if poised at the Gates to Eternity, and conspired with Kastor to falsify the will.

But if I believed killing was wrong, then why did I send Binyamin back to the arena? Another unanswerable question that haunts my daydreams and lurks in the shadows of my insomnia.

The indelible despair, however, was to come later, in the wake of the visit three days ago from Sergius. With his brows rammed together and his voice scraping my ears, he told me what I supposed was inevitable, that death had claimed Binyamin two weeks ago in the Amphitheatre of Pompeii and that the ship bearing his body had just docked in Alexandria. And so, as faithfully as I'd kept my promise to withhold from the authorities my brother's account of Kastor's murder, I prepared a splendid funeral for him at the Great Synagogue and commissioned Sergius to see to the monument.

According to Sergius, Binyamin died without a sigh, his eyes wide open looking fearlessly at death, his face serene. If my brother's knees had buckled when he offered his neck or he'd squirmed when the victor's blade was raised or if the flies had buzzed fiercely in the widening pool of his blood, Sergius made no mention. He said only that Binyamin died as he lived, with pride in the glory of Rome.

And so with the news steeping in my mind, I recalled a family story that had come to define me, the one Aunt Hannah told me about my mother when she was pregnant with Binyamin and me.

"When your mother felt life quicken inside her," my aunt said, "she went to her astrologer, who told her she'd have a daughter with great gifts, one whose contributions would be famous for centuries but who'd also experience great losses."

And so I had. Noah's death thirteen years ago and now Binyamin's, two tragedies that had stained my soul but oddly enough, had also brought me a measure of relief. I only hoped the Almighty would forgive me once again and give my relationship with Judah the chance to prosper before my sweetheart's hair turned completely white.

So far, the Fates had made that impossible.

In the meantime, I continued to dedicate my life to alchemy. During these past three years, I'd been experimenting further with the white herb of the mountain, the fern with the potential to heal, rejuvenate, and extend human life. I'd yet to record the active agent or my method for extracting it, but I'd been administering small doses to Amram regularly. With each passing week, he was becoming more vital. His color has brightened, his mind sharpened, and his once-skeletal frame had filled out. Ironically, if Binyamin had seen Amram as he was now, that devilish scheme to appropriate that dear man's wealth would never have occurred to him.

So, I chose to remember Binyamin as he used to be. And though far from fanciful, I experienced a moment of pleasure now and then when I caught sight of his boyhood face on a lad in the agora or I heard him calling to me when a mule cart on the Canopic Way clattered over the pavement. And so he was here, even though he was not.

May the Almighty repair and shelter the crumpled soul of my dear brother. May he instill in that soul the sense of worth that never came from his Earthly father for only He can fix a broken childhood. And may He continue to bless my work and instruct me in His divine art.

With gratitude to Our Creator,

Μιριαμ βατ Ισααχ

Alexandria *ad Aegyptum*

Summer of the Fifth Year of the Reign of Nero Claudius Caesar Augustus Germanicus

## Author's Note

Did Miriam bat Isaac (aka Maria Hebrea) really identify an ingredient in the fern from which she could synthesize the elixir? If she did, we have no record of it. Still the search for it among Alexandrian alchemists was indeed real.

Likewise, Chinese alchemists independently sought longevity in something they too could ingest. Having observed its immutability, they believed gold to be the miraculous substance. And so, given its scarcity and their poverty, they attempted to synthesize it. Their first known work devoted exclusively to alchemy, the *Ts'an t'ung ch'i* by Wei Po-yang, appeared in 142 CE. But unlike the Alexandrians, the Chinese focused on not only the synthesis of gold from base metals but methods for ingesting it to achieve immortality (Leicester, 1971).

The mythical substance they sought has come to be known as the philospher's stone. Miriam believed that Adam acquired knowledge of the stone directly from the Lord. Studying a particular kind of fern, the white herb of the mountain, *Botrychium lunaria*, she hoped to identify the stone (Patai, 1994).

The search has continued for over two thousand years. Isaac Newton himself, unbeknown to his colleagues, studied alchemy, then known as chymistry. Intent on identifying the philosopher's stone, he wrote about a million words on the subject over the course of his thirty years of research (Newman, 2010). Likewise, today's scientists study our genetic code for the secrets to heal, rejuvenate, and extend human life.

Miriam's success in synthesizing the elixir is my only deliberate departure from the historical record. Careful readers, however, might recognize other instances in which the details of my story run counter to some scholars' claims. For example, according to Quennell (1971), the left index finger was raised to appeal for mercy, whereas in accord with Shadrake (2005), I write that gladiators surrendered by raising the index finger of their right hand.

Similarly, there are conflicting claims as to whether a right-handed *retiarius* threw his net with the left or right hand and even how the mythological ferryman "Charon" was dressed in the arena. These inconsistencies are more likely due to variations in local customs, especially in the outlying provinces, than to scholar errors.

Thus, aside from Miriam's report that she discovered the philosopher's stone, the characters, events, and description in this novel, though narrative inventions, are based on a faithful attempt to interpret the following scholarly works:


Capponi, L. (2011). *Roman Egypt*. New York: Bristol Classical Press.

Casson, L. (1971). *Ships and seamanship in the Ancient World*. Princeton, NJ: Princeton University Press.

Casson, L. (1994). *Travel in the Ancient World.* Baltimore, MD: Johns Hopkins University Press.

Holum, K. G., Hohlfelder, R. L., Bull, R. J., & Raban, A. (1988). *King Herod's dream: Caesarea on the sea.* New York: W. W. Norton.

Korb, S. (2010). *Life in Year One: What the world was like in first-century Palestine.* New York: Riverhead Books.

Kraemer, Ross S. (1998). Jewish Women in the Diaspora World of Late Antiquity. In Judith R. Baskin (Ed.), *Jewish women in historical perspective* (pp. 46—72). (2nd ed.). Detroit, MI: Wayne State University Press.

Leicester, H. M. (1971). *The historical background of chemistry.* New York: Dover.

Levine, L. I. (1975). *Caesarea under Roman Rule.* Leiden, the Netherlands: E. J. Brill.

Lewis, N. (1983). *Life in Egypt under Roman rule.* New York: Oxford University Press.

Lyle, D. P. (2008). *Forensics: A guide for writers.* Cincinnati, OH: Writer's Digest Books.

Marlowe, J. (1971). *The golden age of Alexandria.* London: Victor Gollancz.

Meijer, F. (2004). *The gladiators: History's most deadly sport* (L. Waters, Trans.) New York: Thomas Dunne Books, St. Martin Press.

Newman, W. R. (October 6, 2010). *Why did Isaac Newton believe in alchemy?* Lecture delivered at the Perimeter Institute. Waterloo, Ontario. [available:

podbay.fm/show/129166905/e/1291978800?autostart=1]

Nossov, K. (2009). *Gladiator: The complete guide to Ancient Rome's bloody fighters.* Guilford, CT: Lyons Press.

Patai, R. (1994). *The Jewish alchemists: A history and source book.* Princeton, NJ: Princeton University Press.

Porter, R. (1997). *The greatest benefit to mankind: A medical history of humanity.* New York: W. W. Norton.

Quennell, P. (1971). *Colosseum.* New York: Newsweek Book Division.

Rops, H. D. (1962). *Daily life in Palestine at the time of Christ.* (P. O'Brian, Trans.). London: Phoenix Press.

Shadrake, S. (2005). *The world of the gladiator.* Stroud, Gloucestershire, UK: Tempus Publishing Ltd.

Sly, D. I. (1996). *Philo's Alexandria.* London: Routledge.

Smallwood, E. M. (1976). *The Jews under Roman rule: From Pompey to Diocletian.* Leiden, the Netherlands: E. J. Brill.

## Glossary

*Arenarii* (Latin) ~ the slaves who attend to the arena

*Auctoratus* (Latin) ~ a hired gladiator, trained and obligated by contract to perform for a specified period of time. *Auctoratti* (pl.)

*Balneae* (Latin) ~ small, privately owned bathhouses

*Bibliopōleion* (Greek) ~ bookshop

*Calamistrum* (Latin) ~ curling iron

*Calamus* (Latin) ~ a pen made from bronze or more commonly from a reed cut at an angle and then split. *Calami* (pl.)

*Calceus* (Latin) ~ Roman boot-like shoe worn outdoors; had covered toes and straps extending to the ankle, calf, or knee. *Calcei* (pl.)

*Cantharus* (Latin) ~ an earthenware, the two-handled drinking cup

Capitium (Latin) ~ a short, light chemise used as a woman's undergarment or for sleeping

*Cardo Maximus* (Latin) ~ the main north-south thoroughfare in a Roman city or military camp, in this case Caesarea

*Caupona* (Latin) ~ a low-class hostelry serving carters, sailors, and slaves

*Cauponaria* (Latin) ~ the female innkeeper of a low-class hostelry serving carters, sailors, and slaves

*Cella* (Latin) ~ a garret room or mean apartment. *Cellae* (pl.)

*Cena libera* (Latin) ~ feast given for the participants in a gladiatorial performance on the eve of the games

*Collegium iuvenum* (Latin) ~ a social club for training high-ranking males over the age of fourteen in the martial arts

*Colobium* (Latin) ~ a coarse, short-sleeved, workingman's tunic

*Corbita* (Latin) ~ literally a "basket," refers here to a wide sailing ship with a rounded, big-bellied hull for cargo

*Corona* (Latin) ~ the laurel wreath, the ultimate award to a gladiator for an exceptional bout

*Cubiculum* (Latin) ~ a sleeping chamber

*Cupido victoriae* (Latin) ~ the desire to win, one of the virtues gladiators were expected to demonstrate in the arena

*Damnatio ad bestias* (Latin) ~ literally "condemnation to beasts," refers to a form of public execution for common criminals in which the condemned was torn to pieces in the arena by wild beasts.

*Diliad, The* (Greek) ~ a parody of *The Iliad* mentioned in *Aristotle's Poetics*

*Diolkos* (Greek) ~ the paved ramp constructed in Ancient Greece to drag ships across the Isthmus of Corinth

*Dolos* (Greek) ~ the Greek god of trickery, fraud, and deception

*Doctor* (Latin) ~ a trainer of gladiators in a gladiatorial school. *Doctores* (pl.)

*Editor* (Latin) ~ organizer of gladiatorial games

*Familia gladiatoria* (Latin) ~ a troupe of gladiators coming from the same school

*Habet!* (Latin) ~ literally "He's done for," the noisy cry of spectators at the sign of a gladiator's defeat

*Henket* (derived from Egyptian) ~ a cheap Egyptian beer made from barley or emmer wheat

*Hoc habet!* (Latin) ~ literally "Now he's had it," the noisy cry of spectators at the sign of a gladiator's defeat

*Hypogeum* (Greek) ~ literally "underground," refers to the vast network of cells, chambers, and tunnels in a stadium below the arena

*Instita* (Latin) ~ a wide, Roman-style ornamental flounce or border sewn to the lower hem of a lady's *tunica interior* or *stola*

*Iugula!* (Latin) ~ literally, "Slit his throat," the shout of spectators calling for the death of the gladiator

*Jugula, verbera, ure!* (Latin) ~ literally "Cut, beat, burn," the shout of spectators calling for the death of a defeated gladiator

*Kapēleion* (Greek) ~ a snack bar providing cold snacks and beverages. *Kapēleia* (pl.)

*Lacerna* (Latin) ~ a long, woolen cloak worn by all classes. Those of the wealthy were brightly colored.

*Lanista* (Latin) ~ manager of gladiators in a *familia gladiatorial*. *Lanistae* (pl.)

*Laographia* (Latin) ~ the poll tax levied on all males (slaves included) between the ages of fourteen and sixty, except those belonging to a privileged class, e.g., Roman citizens, priests, scholars in the Museum, and non-Roman, high-ranking officials

*Libitinarii* (Latin) ~ arena slaves in bright tunics who clear the sand and cart off the dead between bouts

*Ludus* (Latin) ~ a training school for gladiators; *ludi* (pl.)

*Megillah* (Hebrew) ~ literally a scroll, refers here to a long and complicated story

*Merda* (Latin) ~ a profane word roughly translated as manure

*Missum!* (Latin) ~ literally "Send him back (to the *ludus*)," the spectators' cry at the end of a bout to spare the defeated gladiator's life

*Mitte!* (Latin) ~ literally "Let him go," the spectators' cry at the end of a bout to spare the defeated gladiator's life

*Novus auctoratus* (Latin) ~ a newly hired gladiator

*Noxi* (Latin) ~ a criminal condemned to death who was either executed or forced to fight to the death in the arena. *Noxii* (pl.)

*Pankration* (Greek) ~ a strenuous sport that combines boxing and wrestling

*Pantopoleion* (Greek) ~ a general store

*Pedisequi* (Latin) ~ the slaves who follow their master when he leaves the house, typically accompanying his litter to secure its safety. One duty is to part the crowds so as to make way for the bearers.

*Pompa* (Latin) ~ the colorful parade preceding the gladiatorial games during which the gladiators enter the arena

*Porta Sanavivaria* (Latin) ~ literally "The Gate of Life," refers to the gate through which the gladiators enter the arena and through which those who have been defeated but spared exit the arena

*Porta Triumphalis* (Latin) ~ literally "The Gate of Triumph," refers to the gate through which the victorious gladiators exit the arena

*Posca* (derived from both Lain and Greek) ~ a spoiled, watered-down wine

*Praegenarii* (Latin) ~ the dwarfed, crippled, and/or deformed men who, with wooden weapons and ludicrous antics, mock the gladiators to amuse the spectators

*Primus palus* (Latin) ~ literally "the first pole," refers to the highest of the four ranks of gladiators in a *familia gladiatoria* based on the gladiator's record of bouts and victories

*Prolusio* (Latin) ~ the preliminary gladiatorial combat with blunt weapons

*Retiarius* (Latin) ~ the only type of gladiator to fight without a helmet, specialized in using a net and trident as his weaponry, trained to fight a *secutor. Retiarii* (pl.)

*Rudis* (Latin) ~ the wooden sword that symbolizes a volunteer gladiator's discharge from his contract

*Sagina* (Latin) ~ barley stew, the staple of a gladiator's diet

*Secutor* (Latin) ~ the kind of gladiator who fights a *retiarius*. His equipment includes a helmet, shield, and sword. *Secutores* (pl.)

*Sestertii* (Latin) ~ large brass Roman coins worth about two loaves of bread each

*Shabbat* (Hebrew) ~ the Sabbath, the seventh day of the Jewish week, a day of rest observed from a few minutes before sunset on Friday to a few minutes after three stars appear in the sky on Saturday night

*Sica* (Latin) ~ a short, curved dagger used by the *Sicarii* and the type of gladiator known as a *thraex*. *Sicae* (pl.)

*Sicarii* (Latin) ~ assassins belonging to a secret brotherhood named for the daggers, the *sicae*, they conceal under their cloaks

*Spoliarium* (Latin) ~ the pit below the arena where the bodies of slain beasts and gladiators are dumped to await mass burial

*Stoa* (Greek) ~ a long, low building with a columned porch facing the center of the agora

*Stola* (Latin) ~ the traditional, boxy outer tunic married women wear.

*Sukkot* (Hebrew) ~ The Feast of Booths, a biblical Jewish holiday observed on the fifteenth day of the month of *Tishrei*, sometime between late September and late October

*Summum supplicium* (Latin) ~ the most extreme punishment

*Tessera* (Latin) ~ ticket or token to the games. *Tesserae* (pl.)

*Torah* (Hebrew) ~ the *Pentateuch*, the Five Books of Moses, the foundation of all Jewish legal and ethical precepts

*Tribunal* (Latin) ~ a raised platform for seating dignitaries

*Tunica interior* (Latin) ~ the fitted undergarment a woman wore under her outer tunic (*tunica exterior*)

*Velarium* (Latin) ~ the sailcloth awning that specially recruited sailors extend or retract over the spectators as the sun moves around the stadium or hippodrome

*Veteranus* (Latin) ~ a veteran, such as a trained gladiator

*Via Appia* (Latin) ~ an early and strategically important

Roman road connecting Rome to Brindisi, Apulia in southeast Italy

## About the Author

June Trop and her twin sister Gail wrote their first story, "The Steam Shavel [sic]," when they were six years old, growing up in rural New Jersey. They sold it to their brother Everett for two cents. "I don't remember how I spent my share," Trop says. "You could buy a fistful of candy for a penny in those days, but ever since then, I wanted to be a writer."

As an award-winning middle school science teacher, Trop used storytelling to capture her students' imagination and interest in scientific concepts. Years later as a professor of teacher education, she focused her research on the practical knowledge teachers construct and communicate through storytelling. Her first book, *From Lesson Plans to Power Struggles* (Corwin Press, 2009), is based on the stories new teachers told about their first classroom experiences.

Now associate professor *emerita* at the State University of New York at New Paltz, she devotes her time to writing *The Miriam bat Isaac Mystery Series*. Her heroine is based on the personage of Maria Hebrea, the legendary founder of Western alchemy, who developed the concepts and apparatus alchemists and chemists would use for 1500 years.

Trop lives with her husband Paul Zuckerman in New Paltz, where she is breathlessly recording her plucky heroine's next life-or-death exploit.

CPSIA information can be obtained
at www.ICGtesting.com
Printed in the USA
LVOW03s0019160218
566741LV00010B/592/P